The Montgomery Family Chronicles, Book 3:

A Family Portrait

By J.J. Massa

The Montgomery Family Chronicles, Book 3, A Family Portrait,
J.J. Massa Copyright © 2010, 2011
ISBN 978-1-61235-148-3

Credits

Editor: Mae Powers
Copy Editor: Taylor Evans
Cover Artist: A.Bratt

The Montgomery Family Chronicles
Book 3: A Family Portrait

By J.J. Massa

Tavist Darke lost his mate and pup years ago and never expected to have a family. He no longer looked for happiness in life. He didn't expect to find another mate. The love of his adopted pack was more than he ever expected. When he met beautiful Tracey West and her enchanting children he knew his secret prayers had been answered.

Tracey West had a family and she would keep them safe at all costs. She didn't want another mate. She'd been married for almost a decade and had three beautiful and special children as a result. Living in and getting out of that marriage had been a nightmare. All she wanted now was peace and safety for herself and her kids. Why couldn't her sexy neighbor understand that?

www.jjmassa.com

Also by JJ Massa:
Mélange Digest, Short Story: Nailed
Vampire Anthology: Slow Burn
Vampire Novel: Counting Midnight
Vampire Anthology: Dark Blood

The Montgomery Family Chronicles: (Werewolf Series)
Book 1, Acting Like Family
Book 2, Family Harmony

The Montgomery Family Chronicles
Book 3: A Family Portrait
By J.J. Massa

Chapter 1

Tavist Darke stood deep in the woods watching as one of his new neighbors got off the bus. He recognized the child's scent. Her family had rented the small house just past his at the end of the road. He'd kept the agency from naming him as the owner. He would, of course, introduce himself later, if he found a reason to. Theirs were the only two houses here. Tav's house was hidden in the trees with a short path connecting the two homes.

There were other things he'd noticed when he'd gone to check out the new family. He found that no man lived there and fear had moved into that house. One woman lived there, one girl, and two young boys, all very much afraid of something or someone.

As he watched the little girl, he saw that she didn't walk down the middle of the road like most innocent children eager to get home. She was furtive, like a little animal. Her actions reminded him of tiny mice, rabbits, even small birds that so cautiously peek out and very carefully make their way from safe haven to safe haven.

Predators were everywhere, of course; he knew that better than most. During his short military career, he'd been stationed in Somalia and other distant, war torn places where he'd served his country. The children, the mothers, everyone would edge so carefully out of their homes trying to meet various needs and not be noticed or attacked. It broke his heart that the most innocent of the world's citizens had to live in fear. He couldn't help but wonder what had inspired such caution in this particular child.

Today, it seemed, the little girl was right to be cautious. She *was* being stalked. From behind her came two boys who were a little older than her seven or eight years. One boy pushed her down and the other grabbed her backpack and dumped it out.

"Go home, new kid! Go back where you came from," they sneered, chanting in unison.

The larger of the boys had begun to kick at her when Tav grabbed them by the backs of their necks and lifted them into his face. They were Were pups.

"Go home. Tell your Mamas and Daddies that I was mean to you. Tell them to come and talk to me. They'd better bring the Sheriff. It's not safe to walk down this road if you don't live here," he growled, dropping the two miscreants.

The young werewolf boys didn't wait to hear more. The older of the two choked out a broken, "yessir," as he whirled and ran back up the gravel road, toward the bus stop. His cohort dashed up behind him and soon, they were out of sight.

If the Sheriff came, that was fine. He was a werewolf, too. He and Tav understood one another very well. Tav would not interfere with his pack or issue a pack challenge. Tav's territory began at the southern edge of town and consisted of the forty acres he lived on. He owned the only two houses on the property.

Turning back to the little girl, Tav dropped to one knee. She was struggling to hold back her tears and contain her fear. His heart melted. Without speaking, he began to gather her books, papers and pencils and stuff them back into her backpack.

Handing it to her, he noticed that her knee was scraped up with gravel from the road. He pulled out his handkerchief and began to dab at it.

"N-no, mister, I'm, I'm okay," she stuttered, jerking away from his care. "I gotta get home. M-Mama'll be worried!" She scrambled backward and ran.

He listened to her progress and heard her stop much sooner than she should have. If he wasn't mistaken – he lifted his nose to the air – yep, she was standing in the trees on the right. Nowhere near her house. Was she trying to throw him off? How did a young child like this one know anything about misleading a grownup in such a way?

Tav decided to wait. He sat in the dirt at the side of the road and just listened to the rooting and chirping of small animals that lived in the woods on either side. He kept his attention on the little girl who was finally resuming her journey home from the bus stop.

Closing his eyes, he pictured her coming into her yard and running up the steps to her porch. He imagined her throwing open the door to her house and calling out for her mother.

Emotions strong and painful seemed to hit him square in the chest in an unexpected blow to his heart. He wrapped both arms around his middle and doubled over. If he hadn't been sitting, he would have been driven to his knees.

Tate, his little boy, would have been that girl's age if he'd lived, he realized. He would have had dark hair like hers, and pretty dark eyes. Grief overwhelmed him. In the seven years since the death of his mate and pup, the hurt hadn't lessened. How he missed the feel of that warm little body squirming in his arms. Tav closed his eyes and imagined the last time he'd seen his son alive.

The little boy had been so proud of himself – he'd put his own shoes on that morning. His mother, Kylie, had been rushing around the house, anxious to drop Tate off at daycare so that she could meet with some gallery owners that wanted Tav's work. She felt it was important that Tate socialize with other children and drove him every day.. Tav missed him, both of them, so much. He howled low in his throat, still mourning his family.

After a minute, Tav began to climb to his feet. That's when he saw it. It was a letter sized square of cardstock. Turning it over, he saw a gold leaf seal and read:

Certificate of Recognition
In Appreciation of the Best Spelling Grade
Ashley West
Is presented with this prestigious award
Presented by:

Certificate # LMH 46258465411   Merlinda Eugene
                                        Third Grade Teacher

Tav smiled to himself. This was too important a document not to return to her. No doubt little Ashley West would be very disappointed if she couldn't share her success with her mother. The remembered pain eased at the thought of the child's pride in her accomplishment. The world seemed a slightly brighter place with evidence of her success.

Still smiling, Tav walked up the dirt driveway and into the yard in front of little Ashley's house. He heard a movement to his right and glanced over in time to see a very small boy rounding the corner of the house.

From inside the house, Tav heard a woman's voice saying, "I've got to go, Sue. The best looking man I've ever seen in my life just strolled into my front yard and he's going to scare my children half to death any minute now."

Catching sight of Tav, the little guy emitted a squawk of surprise, and plopping down on his tiny bottom, began to howl.

"Shut up, ya big baby! C'mon, Christopher, don't be a tattletale, Mom's gonna hear…" An older boy, older than the toddler, anyway, had just raced around to the front of the house. He hit the brakes when he spotted Tav. "Mom!" came his strangled shout. "Mo-om!"

Both children were apparently frozen in fear. The fear scent was punctuated by the urine smell of the youngest boy giving in to nature's call.

He heard the sound of a phone being placed on its hook and then approaching footsteps. Werewolf hearing was both a gift and a curse. The screen door opened and a woman stepped out. For the second time in less than an hour, Tav felt the air whoosh from his lungs as if he'd fallen flat on his back from a great height.

"Into the house boys!" the little flame haired titan snapped. "Now." She said it evenly but that one word mobilized the two frozen boys. As they scampered behind her and through the front door, she trained her icy blue gaze on Tav. "Help you, mister?"

How can her eyes look icy and hot at the same time? The part of his brain that handled motor skills came to his rescue. He stepped forward and extended the hand holding Ashley's certificate of recognition. He couldn't remember the last time he'd felt so awkward around someone.

Her eyes never left his face as she rested one hand on the porch railing and reached out for the document. Looking down, her lush mouth curved into a beautiful smile. So beautiful that, just when he thought he could draw a breath into his lungs, the air rushed from them again.

"Oh thank you, mister! Ashley is going to be so happy!" she began to turn and the railing she was holding gave out.

She'd been half turned away from him and holding the railing for support. Now, her arms pin-wheeling wildly, she fell, right into his waiting embrace.

When his chest began to burn, Tav found that, for some reason, his lungs had apparently volunteered to stop working. Taking a deep breath, he struggled to regain his equilibrium. *Cinnamon rolls, apple blossoms, vanilla beans – man she smells good!* Tav resisted the urge to bury his face in the satin waves of fire colored hair just under his chin.

Must let go! Must relax arms! Must release woman. Must. let. go. of. woman!

"Are you okay, ma'am?" he managed, clearing his throat. He'd relaxed his arms, but he didn't release her. That was fair enough because she was still clinging to him, trembling.

"I think so…"

Did she realize that her nose was buried in the vee of his shirt? He could feel her eyelashes tickling his sternum when she closed her eyes. Tav angled his pelvis a little so that his hip was touching her abdomen. If he stood flush against her, his erection would probably knock her down.

Reluctantly, he eased her to sit on the edge of the high porch. She seemed a little stunned.

He looked over her head at the little girl standing just inside the door. "Ashley? Would you bring me a wet towel or washcloth?"

He heard the scurry of small feet, the hollow sound of water running, and then she was back. Shyly, the little girl came just to arm's length and handed him the washcloth. Immediately, she backed away.

"I'm Tavist Darke, by the way," he told the woman, wiping the blood away from the deep scratch on her arm. "Do you have any antibiotic ointment? Gauze?"

The red-haired goddess jerked from his touch. "I'll put something on it when I go inside. Thanks for all your help, Mr. Darke." She had apparently gotten over being stunned.

"When we come to fix the porch in the morning, my buddies Marc or T. Paul can look at your arm. They're both doctors," he explained.

"Thank you for your concern, Mr. Darke," she growled, her tone frosty. *Whew, she's hot.* "It won't be necessary for you or your friends to fix my porch or look at my arm."

"Okay," he said, easily.

He stepped back and smiled. She probably thought he was agreeing with her. He wasn't – not in the way she was thinking. He was simply acknowledging that it wasn't strictly necessary. He did all kinds of things that weren't necessary.

Of course, as owner, and therefore landlord, it was completely necessary.

* * * *

"What did you think of that guy?" Ashley whispered to Jacob, careful not to wake their youngest brother as she slipped into the low bunk beside him.

"That Darke guy?" he murmured, waking instantly as he always did.

Ashley nodded, waiting patiently. Jacob was almost three years her junior, but he could usually tell who was good and who wasn't. She was more likely to like someone just because they were female or run away from a man, no matter whether he was nice or not.

"I dunno, Ash," he answered finally. "He was awfully big… He seemed okay, but you can't really trust that sometimes, y'know?"

She sighed in disappointment. There would be no easy answers here. "Yeah, I know," she mumbled. "I just wondered what you thought."

"I pretty much try to 'void most big people. You should, too," Jacob advised. "They're un-,un-, well, you just can't tell what they're gonna do next and then it's too late."

Ashley looked at her brother for a long minute. "Yeah, I know," she agreed finally. "It would be so nice if there were more of 'em on our side, though, you know?" She slid off the bed, ready to tiptoe back to her own small room. It wouldn't do to wake up their mother after all the upset earlier.

Chapter 2

Tracey West had gone to bed the night before fuming. She'd gotten up this morning narrow-eyed. She was still grumbling when her best friend Sue arrived in time to drive Ashley to the bus stop.

Sue didn't live close enough anymore to just drop in, but sometimes, she did it anyway. The two women had become firm friends first through email when Tracey had joined an online reader's group and then, upon learning that they lived reasonably close to each other, they managed to meet in person. Not long after that, the two were fast friends.

Sue had supported Tracey during her difficult pregnancy with Christopher, never judging her the times she'd tried to leave Jack, her ex-husband, and failed. Later, after her youngest son Christopher was born, Sue had been there, offering shelter and a shoulder to lean on as Tracey finally pressed charges against Jack and had him put in jail.

These days, she and Sue were closer than sisters and spoke on the phone daily. They now lived only an hour away from each other and both women lamented the distance. Sue had the day off today and came early, planning to leave before supper.

Tracey knew that Sue was merely humoring her and that just made her angrier. Right now, Sue was sitting in a chair listening smugly to her complain about the horrible hunky man with the sexy voice who'd brought her little girl's paper home after saving the child from bullies. After that, the drool-worthy jerk had the audacity to catch her in his muscular arms and care for her injury!

That wasn't bad enough, though. The studly pig had suggested that he'd bring friends and fix the dangerous broken railing. Men! Who did they think they were? Just because he was a famous artist... Well, most likely it was also because he owned the house, which she learned when she'd called the rental agency last night, but she didn't want to think of that now. Sue was openly laughing at her, she could tell.

Something caught Sue's attention and she leaned forward, her gaze fixed on something outside.

"I'll take *that* one!" Sue said firmly, standing and walking to the screen door, pointing into the distance.

"Huh?" Tracey uncurled her diminutive frame from the couch and joined her friend at the door.

"There were three…" Sue mused. "I wonder where the other one went?"

Tracey stood dumbfounded as not one, but two very attractive men were standing in front of her porch holding what could only be porch railings. Forgetting that she was dressed only in her knee length pink sleep shirt emblazoned with the cartoon image of Sweet Polly Purebred, Tracey flung open the door and stomped out.

"*There's* the third hunky guy!" Sue grinned.

A smiling man had been standing by the door, obviously waiting for her. As soon as Tracey stopped moving and put her hands on her hips, he pounced.

"Mornin', ma'am. I'm Dr. T. Paul Fonteneax," he introduced himself, while he removed her makeshift bandage and wiped off the cream she'd applied.

"Hey!" she squealed, then she whipped around to look at Tav.

The man with him seemed to be having a great deal of trouble containing his mirth. In fact, tears were streaming down his face and he turned away.

"This hyena over here is my friend Marc. Marc Fonteneax, meet Ms. West." He had the nerve to smile at her. Smile at her! *How DARE he speak to her in such a sexy voice and smile that intimate bedroom smile at her!*

"Stop that!" she turned and snapped at T. Paul.

"Okay," he grinned. It seemed he had finished anyway.

"What are you doing here?" she growled at Tav.

"I'm fixing the porch railing," he explained patiently.

"I told you not to!" *He doesn't have to look so proud of himself, does he?*

"Actually, ma'am, you said it wasn't *necessary*." His mouth kicked up in a half smile. "You didn't say I couldn't do it."

Tracey looked at Tavist Darke's handsome face. His gray eyes sparkled with humor. He looked like a mischievous little boy with that little half smile. *Okay, not a mischievous little boy, a mischievous BIG boy.*

She whirled around and stomped into the house. Turning toward her friend sharply, Tracey was just in time to see Sue wave at the men as she followed her through the door. Plopping down on the couch, she reached for her coffee. Wisely, Sue didn't say a word.

The women sat in silence listening to the men outside. At first, the sound of Marc Fonteneax finally letting go of his laughter was all that could be heard.

"Oh where, oh where…" he choked, laughing.

"…Has my *Underdog* gone?" his brother guffawed.

"There's no need to fear, Underdog is here!" the two brothers sang, laughing again.

"You two aren't hyenas, you're coyotes!" Tav growled at them in a low, amused voice.

"Brother, if that's Sweet Polly Purebred, I wanna fight crime!" T. Paul spoke up.

"I'm telling Lacey you said that," rumbled Tav.

"Come on, Underdog! Let's sing a song, want to?"

Tracey stood and headed down the hall to check on the boys and change her clothes. Glancing out the window at the end of the hall, she saw Marc throw an arm across Tav's shoulders. T. Paul threw an arm across him on the other side. Both brothers began to sing.

"Speed of lightning, roar of thunder!" They were beginning to laugh again. "Fighting all who rob or plunder!"

Now Tav was laughing unrestrainedly too. "I swear I should've gone back to the zoo!"

Tracey shook her head and joined her boys who were both gathered at their window watching the "Hot Men Laughing Show".

It wasn't long before Sue joined the trio at the window, laughing and elbowing Tracey. "They look like a fun bunch of guys, don't they?" she chuckled.

"Um, I don't know, Aunt Sue," Jacob offered nervously. "They're laughing but they're awfully big."

"Well, buddy," Sue grinned at Jacob and then at Tracey, "No law says great big, good-looking guys can't be a lot of fun, right?"

"Sue," Tracey growled a warning, "What're you up to here?"

"Nothing, for heaven's sake," Sue shot back impatiently. "Look, Tracey, they aren't here to take advantage of you or do anything to the kids. They're over there fixing your porch, woman!"

Tracey heaved a gusty sigh. "Okay, okay, you're right. I'm sure they're just great big good Samaritans. It's just…" she took a deep breath and turned her head, swallowing to keep the niggle of fear under control. "They're strangers, Sue."

"Tracey," Sue moved around beside her friend while the boys continued to watch the men's antics. "What are you teaching your kids by not giving these guys a chance?"

"I'm teaching them caution, Sue," she snapped in an angry whisper.

"They already know how to be cautious, Tracey, you're teaching them to be afraid – to stay afraid – of everybody," Tracey felt a jolt of anger flash through her body.

If it was aimed at herself or her best friend, she wasn't sure.

She took another deep, fortifying breath. "What do you think I should do then?" she gritted.

"How about we keep an eye on them and on the boys without keeping ourselves locked in the house all day? Fair?" Sue looked at her innocently.

"Fair," Tracey growled back with ill grace, snatching up Christopher and heading to the bathroom with him.

Sue, the nagging harpy, followed her down the hall. "Admit it, Tracey, you're attracted."

Tracey rolled her eyes and plopped Christopher down on the toilet seat, doing her best to ignore her friend.

"Attacked, Mama? Gonna get hurt?"

Shaking her head, Tracey exhaled slowly. "Mama's not going to get attacked *or* hurt, promise." She raised her voice and added for Sue's benefit, "I'm in no danger of getting hurt because none of those louts is getting anywhere near me! And I'm *not* attracted."

"Why Tracey West! I cannot believe you would fib so to your own little boy!" Sue nudged open the bathroom door, "How can you expect honesty from your children when you know you're not telling the truth right now? You would have him believe that you dislike that poor man."

"Uh, oh!" Christopher crooned his face a study in shock and disapproval. "Mama's fibbing? *And* being mean*!*" He wagged his pudgy little finger at Tracey sternly. "You could make him sad by saying you don't like him. 'Specially if he likes you, too. That's very bad, Mama. You should tell him "Sorry"."

After leveling a scalding glare at Sue, Tracey knelt down to help Christopher change from his pajamas. "Don't worry, baby, he won't be sad, because I didn't tell him that I don't like him. So there's no fibbing involved, either," she assured the little boy, lifting his shirt off and then washing his face. "You'll have to be nice and let him play with your toys, right?"

"I doubt that I have any toys Mr. Darke would like to play with, honey." When Christopher looked like he wasn't satisfied with this, Tracey quickly added, "If he'd like to read one of my books, I'll share nicely, I promise."

Christopher narrowed his fine blue eyes at his mother, apparently doubting her intention to play nicely. Sue, of course, couldn't mind her own business.

"I'll make sure that Mommy let's Mr. Tav sit on her chair if he wants, or look at all the pretty pictures on the wall," Sue guaranteed smugly.

Turning toward Sue, Tracey let go of Christopher who shot down the hall, calling, "I'm going to put my macaroni picture on the wall that I made yesterday, so he can come and see it. Can I put it on the wall, Mama? I know it's dry!" He was gone before Tracey could even articulate an answer.

"*You* are a pain in my…caboose," Tracey hissed at Sue.

"Tell me you don't like him, Tracey. Pretend you aren't attracted. Come on, convince me," Sue taunted with a smirk.

"Shut up," Tracey grumbled. It was the best she could do.

Chapter 3

"You can tell 'em till you're blue in the face," T. Paul was expounding. "All women think they're fat – every doggone one of 'em. Doesn't matter what you tell 'em. Doctor, artist, whatever, you just cannot convince a woman that she's not fat."

"My mommy's not fat." The men looked over at the small boy edging out the door. "She *thinks* she is, though."

"See what I mean? This young man knows and he's only…How old are you, partner? Twelve? Fourteen?" T. Paul rubbed his chin.

Rolling his eyes, Marc looked over at the little boy. "Don't let him try to make you old before your time, son. He can't be a day over ten years old, T. Paul. I know – I work with kids."

Tav leaned over and whispered, "He works with *babies*, not real kids."

He handed the boy a hammer and pointed to the nail. The little boy grinned widely. Tav felt his heart flip.

"I'm Jacob. I know I don't look like I'm ten." He took the hammer Tav offered him and held it in both hands.

"Want me to hold it with you this first time?" Tav asked him, waiting.

Jacob nodded. Nervously, he edged in front of Tav's legs to be closer to the nail. Together they whacked the nail solidly. The little boy's face shone as if he'd won a medal.

"I'm six," Jacob said, taking the hammer in both hands and tapping the nail. "I'm the man in my family, though."

The three men nodded sagely. "Try it again, Jacob," Tav encouraged him.

Braver this time, the little boy smacked the nail solidly with the hammer. He gave it a good lick but his limited strength didn't allow him to control the hammer. It slid off the nail and hit Tav squarely on the thumb. The little boy dropped the hammer and cringed, petrified. Tav ignored the other two men as well as the two women he knew were standing just inside the door. He cupped the little boy's shoulder and leaned down to his ear.

"Jacob? I'm not mad at you, son," he said quietly. Jacob warily lifted his eyes to Tav's. "Accidents happen. That's why I wear these gloves when I work with tools. Later, we'll go get you some gloves

15

like mine." Jacob's wide eyes were still fixed on Tav's. "A man needs a good pair of gloves when he's working."

"Mr. Darke, I didn't mean to hit your finger," Jacob mumbled.

"If I thought you did mean it, I might get a little mad." He grinned and then his face became serious again. "Jacob, even if I got *real* mad at you, I'd never hit you, okay? You should know that if we're going to be friends. You can call me Tav. That's Mr. Marc and that's Mr. T. Paul."

Tav directed Jacob's attention back to the business of hammering nails again. Out of the corner of his eye, Tav saw Tracey's friend let the youngest boy, who looked to be about three years of age, out onto the porch.

"There's nothing sexier in this whole world than studly guys with kids, huh Tracey?" Tav heard Sue ask her friend.

Tracey…It goes very well with Tavist. Tav and Tracey Darke…Oh, hell, what am I thinking? Oh, but she smells so perfect, and I already love these kids.

He was attracted to her, yes. In fact, he'd fallen for her the moment he laid eyes on her. But more than that, Tav knew this woman was his mate. He had no doubt about it. They were already promised to each other if that was so. Tav decided that he very much wanted her to be his mate. If, in this lifetime, the fates should decide to gift him with a second mate, he was not going to fight it. It looked like he'd have his hands full fighting Tracey.

He laughed outright when he heard Tracey groan in disgust and stomp off. Jacob was busy laughing at Marc. Christopher had him by both ears and was blowing raspberries into his face. Suddenly, it seemed, something occurred to the boy.

"Tav, how come you guys were laughing about Underdog? Don't you like him?" Jacob asked. After a pause, he added, "My mom really loves Underdog."

T. Paul and Marc began to laugh helplessly again.

"We like Underdog a lot, Jacob!" Marc said when the chuckles finally began to abate, started blowing raspberries into Christopher's tummy.

"Course we do!" T. Paul laughed. "We call ol' Tav here Underdog. He rescues damsels and fights evil-doers all the time."

"Momma said last night that you drew pictures and make things to look at and get money for that?" Jacob looked questioningly at Tav.

While Tav hadn't cared for fame and attention in the past, he was glad of it right now, because it told him that Tracey knew of his work and recognized his name. Obvously, it hadn't swayed her in any direction regarding him, but at least she'd talked about him just a little. It made him feel closer to her somehow.

"That is exactly what I do, son. I draw pictures and make things to look at. That's what I do. You stay right here and keep Mr. T. Paul out of trouble. And don't let him tell you any lies. I'll be right back." Tav got up and walked over to the door.

He opened the screen door and looked in. Sue smiled and pointed down the hall. *An ally! I know I'm gonna need a few of those.* She'd been quick, during a lull in the work, to tell Tav to check out all the nice work on the kitchen wall when he had a chance. He'd decided right then to make sure he found a chance.

Tav began heading down the darkened hallway. Tracey who had been gathering laundry, wasn't watching where she was going and walked straight into him.

"We have *got* to keep meeting like this," he grinned, wrapping his arms around her to keep her from staggering backward. *I wouldn't want her to trip.* An armload of bed sheets was pressed between them.

"Mr. Darke, what are you doing here?" Her voice sounded distinctly breathless to him and he could smell the fear she fought so valiantly to hide.

"Here in general?" he asked looking around. "Or here?" he tightened his arms around her.

Tav admired Tracey's strength and her determination not to let him know how nervous she was of him and his friends. He sensed that any man would make her nervous and he wondered why. Thank heavens for Sue. She obviously cared about Tracey, but also recognized that Tav meant her now harm.

"Uhmm…" she squeaked. She cleared her throat.

He leaned down closer, his lips brushing her ear. She'd dressed in threadbare jeans and a cotton shirt. Her vibrant red hair was pulled back in a flame colored ponytail.

He didn't try to resist nuzzling her ear with his lips. Once. Twice. *Mmmm.*

"What do you want, Mr. Darke?" her voice was low and wavering.

The panic she'd been struggling with sounded in her voice. She stood stiff and frozen in his arms, shaking slightly. He wanted her in his arms willingly.

Reluctantly, he loosened his hold on her and stepped back. "I'm going into town to get some sandwiches and I'd like to know what you and your friend would like. I'd like to take Jacob with me. And…" He didn't miss her indrawn breath when he'd told her that he'd like to take her son with him.

"Nothing, no, and what?" she growled at him.

Obviously, giving her some space had been a mistake. "Call me Tav. Or Tavist. Please?" he gave her a little smile.

To his surprise, her eyes filled with tears. "Why are you here?"

He couldn't help it. He stepped forward and gathered her into his arms once again, resting his cheek on her head. "Where else would I be?" he asked.

He felt her try to rub at her face even though her hands were full. Gently, he leaned down and kissed one eyelid and the other. He leaned away from her to look into those beautiful fear-filled blue eyes.

"My friends and I like to fix things. We like kids. You have some broken things and you have kids. I'm your only neighbor. We should look out for each other."

She studied his face for long minutes. "I don't need anyone to look after me. You and your friends can go fix someone else." Her words said she didn't need him but her voice and manner said she did.

"I really need someone to look out for me, though," Tav countered. "And I really need to be able to look out for someone else. I can't help it – it's how I am," he explained apologetically.

"I can't stop you from fixing the porch but that's *all* that needs fixing around here. I'll make lunch." She tugged out of his arms.

Once again he let her go – albeit with difficulty. "You mind if I bring you some food to fix? We eat…we eat a lot. *A lot*." He didn't want to shock her but she might as well find out now.

"A whole lot?" She tilted her head and looked at him. He couldn't believe the inner battle he fought to keep his hands and his lips to himself.

"We're really big guys with high metabolisms." He nodded.

"Okay," she finally conceded.

He turned to leave. He wanted to go and come back. For once, he was very glad that there was a *Super Wal-Mart* nearby.

"Tavist?" Tracey cleared her throat. He had his back to her so she didn't see his sloppy grin.

"Yes, Tracey?" He inclined his head back toward her.

"You aren't going to bring alcohol are you? Like beer?"

He turned to look at her worried face. "No, love. Root Beer is as close as I get. Same with Marc and T. Paul."

"You don't drink?" She seemed nervous about asking him this.

"None of my friends drink, Tracey. We don't need it." She nodded. "Besides," he grinned, "don't you think hammers and nails and beer are a recipe for personal injury?"

She smiled shyly at him. "Yes, I definitely do."

* * * *

Tracey moved to the open window that was nearest Jacob. She listened as Tav stopped to tell the boy he was leaving.

"Jacob, I'll be right back, I'm going to the store to get lunch." He'd stopped and rested a large hand on his small shoulder.

"Tav?" Her son sounded so hopeful. "Can I go with you?"

Tav looked around and then edged Jacob a little few steps away from the other two men and Christopher. Lowering his voice, he asked, "If I take you with me who would look after your mama?" He glanced at T. Paul and Marc. They were taking turns playing with Christopher and working on the railings. "She might be uncomfortable with those two strange jokers hanging around."

Jacob took a deep breath and shoved his hands in his pockets, rocking back on his heels. He nodded sagely. "I guess they're probably harmless," he said. She saw Tav fighting a smile. "Still, they're big and mean lookin'," Jacob said.

Tav squeezed his shoulder and said, "I'll be pretty quick. I need some groceries in my belly, how about you?"

Jacob rocked back on his heels again and said nodding, "A guy's gotta eat."

Tav looked up then and caught her watching them through the window. Tracey had the impression that he'd known she was there the whole time. He was gone a remarkably short time for the amount of food and other things he brought back. Tracey and Sue were in awe of the three pounds of roast beef, three pounds of ham, three pounds of cheese and five pounds of hamburger meat that were in the bags he

19

hauled into the kitchen. He told her that he wasn't sure what kind of condiments she, Sue, and the boys liked so he got mayonnaise, mustard, catsup, and salad dressing. He'd also gotten rolls, bread and buns of various descriptions.

She was surprised to find three gallons of milk in the bags. "Don't be shy about making plenty. I meant what I told you, we eat a *LOT*." *Was he blushing?*

* * * *

Everybody spread out on the porch, picnic style and ate. It was a nice day and there really wasn't room in the house. Tracey had cooked up half the meat in rare and medium rare burgers for the men and Sue had piled meats and cheeses on ten of the rolls.

Christopher was dividing his time between the bread and lunchmeat that she and Sue were trying to feed him and the plastic hammer and nail set Tav had brought him. He'd given Jacob a small pair of leather work-gloves, a smaller hammer, and a couple of different "smart nail holders" for them to try. She'd seen him place a nice frame on Ashley's bed for her award certificate.

Date behavior and we're not even dating. He's not going to get to me. No he isn't. I cannot be swayed. Just because he makes me feel like a teenager, a pretty *teenager…No, I can't just trust a guy because he's hot, sensitive, likes children, has strong arms, and makes me feel safe.*

Tracey groaned under her breath.

"So do you guys live nearby, too?" Sue asked Marc and T. Paul after nudging Tracey with an elbow. A vegetarian, Sue was eating a roll stuffed with cheese, breaking off pieces for Christopher when he toddled over.

"Nope," said T. Paul. "I live in Baton Rouge where we grew up."

"I live in Tampa," said Marc.

"How'd you guys meet? In college?" Sue was ever curious. So was Tracey but she wasn't going to admit it.

The men laughed. "Nope!" laughed T. Paul. "You think this ignorant hound went to college?" He gave Tav's shoulder a shove. "He spent his college years out saving the world."

Tracey would have liked to hear more about that but Sue was asking the questions.

"So?" Sue drawled. "How *did* you meet?"

"Through one very special lady," declared Marc. Tav reached over and squeezed his shoulder. "I delivered her babies. Twins." All of the sudden Marc was intensely interested in Christopher again, snatching him up and rubbing his face on the little boy's tummy.

"They got a bad virus in Baton Rouge. They would've died if we hadn't caught it in time. That's when I met Tav," T. Paul explained. "But Tav had the toughest gig."

"What was that?" Tracey had to ask, noticing Tav shaking his head from side to side.

"My buddy here came out of hiding to keep her safe until she could get with her mate – her husband," Marc told them.

"Why was that such a difficult job?" Sue asked. "And why would you think you had to do it?"

"Underdog here," Marc reached over and squeezed Tav's neck affectionately, "saw our friend and her little boys being attacked. He scared the a—animal away and stayed with her for a year, in the background mostly, until it was over. He even went with her mate to hunt the dirt bag down when he snatched her and one of the pups."

Pups? She and Sue exchanged glances and raised eyebrows. *These guys definitely had an over-the-top canine fixation.*

Tracey couldn't help but be drawn to her sexy neighbor-slash-landlord and his very attractive cohorts. Of the two doctors, it seemed that Tav was closer to Marc. It was obvious to Tracey that Marc thought a lot of Tav in return.

Marc moved over to Christopher's toy to play with him. With a sad sigh, Tav and T. Paul looked at each other and then looked over at Marc. There was a story there, Tracey knew. Did she care enough to find out what it was? She'd always been a little too curious…

"Hey!" T. Paul spoke up. "Listen, let's change the subject. How did you two meet?" he asked the women.

Tracey had about a zillion more questions to ask but she couldn't miss the non-verbal cues. Marc really didn't want to pursue the subject and his friends were looking after him.

"Um…" she searched for the right answer. Sue, the goofball, bailed her out.

"Ours was the quintessential online romance," she sighed, lifting Tracey's hand and kissing it.

Jacob leaned close to Tav. "They think they're cute," he murmured. Tav chuckled.

"They *are* cute, buddy," he answered.

"Guess that's why they think so then!" Jacob shrugged and stood up, first carrying his paper plate to the trashcan before examining his gloves, hammer, and nail holders again.

"Sue owns an online book review magazine. I'm one of the reviewers that write for her," Tracey began to explain.

"How does that work?" Tav wondered, looking from one to the other.

"Authors and publishers advertise with her and I read books and send in my reviews," Tracey explained.

"So you get paid to read books, say what you think, and then report about if you like 'em or not?" T. Paul marveled.

"Yeah! Pretty cool, huh?" she said impishly. "I don't even have to buy the books. I just read 'em and type up what I think."

"Wonder where I can get a job like that?" Sue laughed, picking up some of the lunch litter.

Tracey was amazed at the amount of food the three men packed away. "Did you guys get enough?"

"Can I bring some cookies out, Mom?" Jacob spoke up before anyone could answer Tracey. "Aunt Sue always brings tons of cookies. She likes to cook 'em and we like to eat 'em!"

"I'll bring them out," Sue said, laughing. "I've got to make sure there's a couple left for Ashley!"

Tracey noticed Jacob's worried frown as she went to collect a cranky Christopher from the Fonteneax brothers. She could have sworn one of them said something about how he packed a hell of a wallop for a human pup. *And why is this man referring to my baby as a pup? A HUMAN pup no less!*

The two doctors had resumed their porch repair duties with cookies in hand and Sue in tow. Her favorite motto was "It's free to look!" and she was taking advantage of the bargain.

Tracey had moved to close the window when she realized that Jacob had pulled Tav over near the boys' bedroom window to talk. It was the farthest point on the porch from the pounding.

"Tav," Jacob began, "You know I like you and the guys, right?" Tracey wondered what this was about. She was a little uneasy that Jacob liked the dark haired man already.

"Thanks, Jacob." Tav had squatted down to talk to him. "That really means a lot to me. I like you, too."

"I've got a little problem, Tav." Jacob sounded kind of nervous now, but determined to say what was on his mind.

"You know, Jacob, I want to be your very good friend. Your problem is my problem. Tell me what I can do to help."

"I don't want to hurt your feelings or – or" he cringed a little, "make you mad." Tracey was seriously concerned now.

"Okay, I get that you're really bothered about something and you think I'll take it the wrong way?" Tav asked. Tracey could see her son nodding. "Tell me and we'll work it out like men do, okay?"

Jacob blew out a sigh. "Ashley saw you yesterday. She could probably get used to you after a while." Tav nodded. Jacob looked down at his shoes and back up at Tav. "If she sees all three of you giant guys here when she comes home, she's gonna freak." He closed his eyes and screwed up his face as if expecting a blow to fall.

Surprising Tracey, as well as Jacob from the look on his face, Tav pulled the little boy into his arms for a quick hug. "*You* are a good man, Jacob West. And you're a great brother. I'm proud of you for looking after your sister that way." Tav shook the bemused boy's hand. "I'll make sure I clear those big apes out of here before Ashley gets home."

Jacob beamed up at Tav. Clearly he had found a new hero and best friend and Tracey wasn't sure how she felt about that turn of events. Yes, she wanted her son to have a man to look up to, of course she did. Her problem was that she wasn't even sure how she felt about the sexy stranger that brought his friends to repair her porch.

Chapter 4

True to his word, Tav and the Doctors Fonteneax finished their work and said their goodbyes. They were sitting on Tav's back porch when they heard Sue and Jacob walking up the lane to meet Ashley.

"So you had a good day, huh, little buddy?" they heard Sue ask Jacob.

"I did, Aunt Sue." Jacob's voice dropped a little. "I accidentally hit Tav's finger with a hammer and he didn't even hit me. Not once." The little boy's voice held awe and wonder.

The three werewolves listening exchanged glances.

"You know what, Jacob?" Sue asked.

"What, Aunt Sue?"

"*Most* grown up men don't hit their little boys when accidents happen." This seemed to be a foreign but wondrous concept to the little boy.

"How come my daddy hit me then? And Ashley too, and she never did any accidents?"

Tav felt his teeth lengthen upon hearing this. That anyone would hit either of those children enraged him. The idea that a father who was lucky enough to have his children around him would hit them at all – especially just for the hell of it – it made him crazy. He struggled to contain himself. Looking over, he saw the other two men fighting the same battle.

"Your daddy was – is – he is a bad guy. I don't know what made him that way but you're not like that and I don't think Tav is like that either." Sue was obviously trying to explain the unexplainable to this six-year-old boy.

"Aunt Sue, Daddy said Mama made him that way. Is that why Mama won't hardly talk to Tav? Is she afraid she's gonna make *him* that way, too?"

Tav couldn't contain the snarl of rage that ripped through him. *Where is that bastard? I'll kill him I swear I will.*

"Calm down, man – calm down both of you!" T. Paul rumbled. "I think we need to hear this."

Tav looked at Marc, who was having difficulty controlling his beast, too. Taking deep breaths, he tried to calm himself and listen to the conversation between the woman and the child.

They could hear Sue clearing her throat repeatedly. She was obviously having her own troubles dealing with Jacob's innocent question.

"First of all, little buddy, your daddy only said those ugly things because – because – he's just bad. Your mother didn't make him that way. A man is either bad or he's not." She sighed. "Remember that cartoon we watched where the cat made it look like the dog broke all the dishes?"

"Yeah. He wanted everyone to think the dog was bad and he was good." Jacob was excited that he understood.

"Your dad said your mama was bad because he didn't want everybody to know that he was really the bad person who did all the things wrong."

"So Tav's not gonna ever be like that? And he won't ever hit me or Ashley or Mom?"

"I don't think Tav will ever hit any of you," Sue confirmed.

"Do you think Mom or Ashley will ever believe that? Do you think they'll always be scared?" Jacob sounded hopeful and worried at the same time.

"I don't know, Jacob, I just don't know. Hey, there's Ashley's bus!"

The three werewolves sat quietly, mulling over the conversation they'd listened to. There was really no point in discussing it, though Tav knew they probably should. It bothered them, deeply, Tav especially. He *knew* that Tracey was his mate, as well as a strong and beautiful soul. The idea that anyone would hurt her or those beautiful, innocent children just raised his hackles. Somehow, he'd find a way to make things better for the little family that lived on his property. Eventually, he hoped, they would become his family. *One step at a time.*

* * * *

It scared her. The last thing she needed was to come to the attention of the locals. If one person knew about you, very soon, everybody knew about you. The less attention she attracted, the better.

Tracey had no idea how her ex-husband knew where she was. She had often wondered where he'd found her address to begin with. The moment he'd been arrested the first time, Tracey had gathered up her babies and ran. But Jack had friends. Many friends.

The man who'd just left was most likely not one of those friends, she knew. Nonetheless, she wanted nothing to do with him. Men meant trouble and she'd had enough trouble to last a lifetime.

"Mom?" Tracey started nervously. The children were supposed to be cleaning up for supper. "Are you okay?"

"I'm fine, honey. Strangers make me nervous and I wasn't expecting company," she confessed with an uneasy smile.

"Yeah," Ashley agreed in a rough whisper. "me too."

"Ashley, he didn't seem…I mean, just because I get nervous sometimes, honey, doesn't mean he's going to do anything."

"I know, Mom," Ashley placated her. "I don't think he'd do anything. I really don't. I just…got a feeling from him, y'know?"

For a moment, she wanted to rant, rave, and stomp her feet. *A feeling? What is that supposed to mean?* Instead, she counted to five slowly, in her head, and released a deep, cleansing breath.

"You got a feeling, did you?" she asked, exaggerated disbelief clear in her voice. "Are you sure it wasn't gas or something?"

Ashley gasped in outrage. "Mo-om! Gas? How could you say that? Of *course* it's not gas!"

"Ashley has gas!" Jacob announced gleefully, from the door of the kitchen.

"Gas! Gas!" Christopher took up the chant.

"Mo-oo-om!" Ashley wailed. "How *could* you?" To Jacob, she shouted, "Shut up, you little…" she paused, trying to find a word. "You cretin!" she shrieked.

Jacob stopped teasing and looked alarmed. "Cretin?"

"Curtin! Jacob's a curtin!" Christopher squealed, clapping his hands with excitement.

"*Cretin!*" Jacob and Ashley shouted as one.

Tracey had to turn away, to hide her amusement. Really, she shouldn't laugh. What she should do is wade in there and mediate, but instead, she left them to it while she sidled into the kitchen to put the tea kettle on. She'd have a cup to relax with and maybe the kids could have some hot chocolate…as long as there wasn't any bloodshed beforehand.

She cocked an ear toward the front room. It had quieted down out there substantially. Either someone was dead or curiosity had won out over sibling rivalry.

Yep, there was Ashley's piping little girl voice explaining the difference between a cretin and a curtain. Tracey shook her head.

What a leap…Never a dull moment around here, no matter how badly she wanted one.

And oh, did Tracey long for those dull moments. But with the sudden appearance of tall, dark and Tavist…she had a bad feeling that her precious dull moments would be pretty scarce from here on out.

Truly, no moment with Tavist Darke in it could ever be considered dull, could it? And while Tracey tried to keep her distance, by the end of the afternoon, she had begun to feel more and more at ease in the man's company…in an ever so slightly infatuated sort of way.

* * * *

A few days after fixing Tracey's porch, Marc and T. Paul had continued on their journey north and Tav was prowling the woods between his place and Tracey's. The three men had visited briefly everyday since the first day and Tav made sure to stop by alone, every evening, just to make sure all was well. The visits were brief and he usually just talked to Tracey or to Jacob—with Tracy looking on, but he was becoming familiar to the little family, a known entity. After seeing his two friends off, Tav was on his way home when he heard what sounded like a child crying.

Without thought, he turned toward the sound. As he came out of the trees at the back of the house, he saw eight-year-old Ashley sitting on the hill beyond the back porch. She was wearing a little quilted robe and slippers, and though it was an unseasonably warm night, he worried that she'd be cold.

Tav walked toward her, still in wolf form. He stopped when he heard her gasp, locking eyes with her, willing her to accept him, not fear him. She looked at him with round, frightened eyes.

"Are you gonna eat me?" she whispered. He shook his head *no*. "Are you gonna bite me?" she asked, just a little louder.

He shook his head *no* again. He walked up to her and sat down in front of her. Even seated, he towered over her slight frame, causing her to crane her head to look up at him. When he felt her relaxing in his presence, he leaned down and licked her cheek. She giggled. He smiled. He licked her other cheek. She giggled again. Tav lay down facing her and looked at her.

"Do you have a name?" she asked him. He nodded. "I met a man the other day and his name sounded like a pet's name."

He tilted his head. When she didn't say anything more, he inched forward and licked her hand and then rubbed it with his head.

"You want to sit next to me?" she asked him. He nodded. She patted the ground beside her and he moved over to warm her. "His name was Tavist Darke. It sounds like a vampire name or a cartoon character, but my brother said to call him Tav. That sounds like a dog, right?"

She looked up at him and he nodded.

"So I can call you Tav? You won't mind?"

He leaned down and licked her ear and nodded. She giggled. Tav decided that Ashley's giggle had to be among his top ten favorite sounds of all time.

"I bet you wonder how come I'm out here, huh Tav?" she said.

He nodded, snuggling closer. It wasn't a cold night, really, but she was small and dressed so thinly.

"I heard Mommy crying before. She was asleep." Ashley turned tear-filled eyes to him. "Promise you won't tell, Tav? Promise?" He tilted his head and when she didn't speak, he nodded. Ashley nodded back and began to speak.

"Daddy used to hit Mommy a lot. He hit me and Jacob, too. But mostly, he hit Mommy. He hit her till he was sure she couldn't leave the house for a long time." Her little chin trembled and she released a deep breath on a sob. Turning her head, she scraped her forearm across her eyes and sniffled daintily.

Tav rumbled a growl deep in his chest. He couldn't help it. *The chicken-hearted bastard!* Ashley's arm stole around him and gave him a hug. He rested his head on top of hers. Ashley took a deep breath and continued.

"Even though Daddy's in jail now, I think he still hits Mommy in her sleep." Ashley began to shake with quiet sobs and she clung to the black wolf.

Awkwardly, Tav rubbed the little girl's back with his large paw wanting to cry and rage at the same time. *What kind of an animal had Tracey been married to? And humans believed that werewolves were beasts and monsters!*

Tav knew that he had a beast inside of him. He remembered the day Riker Montgomery had drawn the beast out of his brother Lakon. Both men were family to him – still there was no good excuse for a man to hurt a woman. None. Tav knew that Lakon would never forgive himself for the injury he'd inflicted on his mate.

Werewolves might be half animal and half man but they didn't beat on their children. When it came to their mates, even a single incident of abuse was a rare thing indeed.

Finally, Ashley began to calm down, her breaths coming in broken hiccups. Tav lay down on his side and she draped herself over him, using him as a furry pillow.

"I never said that out loud before," she sighed, sniffing.

Tav wagged his tail in encouragement. He knew it was important that she talk about this so that she could heal. While he was reasonably sure that Tracey had taken her children to counseling, he knew that no force on earth would make a kid talk before he or she was ready.

His heart reached out to this small child…one he wanted to claim as his own. Along with her brothers and especially their mom. Without a doubt, he knew now that the fates had put Tracey in his path for a reason. They all needed each other…

"Jacob said he hit that other Tav with a hammer and he didn't even get mad." She turned her head to look Tav in the eyes. "He's a great big guy with great big muscles. *He* wouldn't be afraid of my daddy would he?"

Tav shook his head from side to side. *No, he wouldn't. In fact, I'd like to meet him.*

"I bet Daddy wouldn't try to hit Tav."

Tav wagged his tail and curled his lip in a feral smile. *Bring it on, Daddy, I dare you.*

"Bet nobody'd ever hit Mom or Jacob or me, or even baby Christopher with either one of you Tavs around, huh?"

Tav wagged his tail again and licked her cheek. *Nobody will ever hit any one of you again, sweetheart. Not as long as I have a heartbeat. Even if I don't I'll make sure of it. Little girls should be spoiled, not terrorized.*

She pressed against him and made a soft sound, worming her way around until she was comfortable. They sat in silence for long minutes. He was sure the exhausted child would doze off pretty soon.

Nuzzling her neck, Tav confirmed that Ashley had fallen asleep. He let her lay there a little longer. Listening intently, he established that all the occupants of the house were deeply asleep as well.

Satisfied, Tav transformed and lifted Ashley. Quietly he carried her into the house and down the hall to her room. He wanted to be quick. Sadly, his clothes did *not* transform along with him. No matter how innocent the circumstance, he couldn't imagine a mother anywhere who'd accept seeing a naked man carrying her eight-year-old daughter around in the middle of the night.

As he left the room, he spotted Ashley's framed award certificate on the wall by the door and smiled. He *would* look after this family, whether they liked it or not.

* * * *

Tav was in the hallway and almost at the front door when he heard Tracey tossing and turning in her bed. Cautiously, he eased her bedroom door open. She had obviously fallen asleep fresh from the shower. Surveying the scene, Tav saw one towel half wadded, half pinned under the flickering fire of her hair. As his eyes traveled down her body, she turned and the towel that had been wrapped sarong-like around her slid off.

"No, please Jack, no!" she moaned, twisting away from the memory of her attacker.

Almost against his will, Tav moved into the bedroom and sat down next to her. "Shhh, Tracey, Jack will never hurt you again," he promised her, keeping his voice low and as soothing as he could make it.

"Never?" she asked, her voice a frightened whisper. She didn't seem to be awake, but she was responding to him.

"Never, Tracey, you're safe now." Cupping her face, he brushed her forehead with his lips.

"Safe?" She murmured in question, turning her face into his palm.

Her breasts brushed his arm and her nipples hardened. Tav bit back a groan as his already rigid erection began to throb in time with the rise and fall of her beautiful breasts. He'd love to lie down beside her but he couldn't take that chance.

"Safe, Tracey," he reaffirmed.

She rolled onto her back again with a slight smile. "Safe," she breathed, adjusting her legs.

Tav looked down at the nest of flame colored curls at the apex of her thighs. He smoothed his hand lightly over one breast and down to those curls. Of course, he knew better, but he just couldn't help himself. Tracey opened her mouth and a sigh escaped her. She shifted and his fingers skated across the pink flesh poking out of the blaze colored tangle.

"Mmm, Tavist," she sighed.

Well, I never saw that *coming…any of it.*

Tav edged away from her and eased to his feet. She couldn't possibly have known he was there, could she? Of course not, or she would certainly not have been so…what? Eager? Enticing? Whatever, it was clear that she'd been thinking about him—dreaming about him, at least. She'd obviously recognized his voice. Apparently the subconscious impression he'd made was decent. It hadn't struck him how much before, but maybe she somehow recognized that he was her mate? Ashley seemed very empathetic and she had to get it from somewhere. She must recognize him subconsciously. Is that why she'd felt him in her sleep? Now, if only he could figure out how appeal to her while she was *awake…*

It was all he could do to force himself to leave the room.

Chapter 5

Once on his back porch, Tav transformed again. Naked, he strode into his kitchen and paused beside the counter, his mind going a mile a minute.

Tracey had been so beautiful lying there in the moonlight wearing nothing but a towel. He thought about how soft and pink she'd looked, with her soft waves of fire curtaining her face and caressing her pink-tipped breasts. A dusky rose in the firelight, that's what she was.

The nest of tight little curls that covered her sex had drawn him to touch. He wanted so much more. Without realizing it, he'd reached for his still hard and still aching erection. Closing his eyes, Tav imagined parting that copper colored thatch and plunging his finger deep, burying himself in all that pink fire. His cock throbbed and his hand tightened around it as he pumped slowly.

His rhythm increased as he imagined splaying her legs wide and touching that soft pink skin with his tongue, his lips…Harder and harder he pumped as his imagination ran away with him, hips rocking in time with his hand. In his mind, he buried himself deep inside Tracey West and he felt his body tighten. With a loud groan, he came, shooting ropes of pearly semen all over the front of his refrigerator.

No question about it, he had it bad. He had to do something and soon. His mate needed him and he needed her. Perhaps it was time for him to stake his claim? Certainly it was time for him to become a more active part of her life.

As her landlord, it would be simple to find reasons to go to Tracey's house. He'd check the back porch for safety. He'd chop wood for the winter. He'd make sure the bushes didn't crowd her windows. It was his *duty*, after all.

Tav would take his time and develop a meaningful relationship with each of her three children. Over time, Tracey would learn that he wasn't a threat to her. She'd realize before long that he would never hurt her.

Of course, he'd try to touch her as often as he could but he would be careful and considerate. She'd soon get used to his touch and his presence in her life. In time, she'd trust him and depend on him to keep her safe.

After awhile, Tracey would learn to associate him with safety and warmth. He might hug her or touch her, but he'd be sure to keep his physical contacts with her brief, non-threatening. Soon, she'd grow to expect him to touch her. To love her.

All he needed was a chance. That's all he wanted. He'd had his mate and pup snatched out of his life with no warning. He still grieved for them and he always would. His parents had been taken from him the same way.

His life had been returned to him that day, about four years ago, when he'd seen his adopted brother's mate, Bethany at the zoo with her pups. August Livingston's attack on the mother and her babies had outraged Tav. He'd been too incensed to lay back and let life happen around him any longer. Out in the world were people, people and werewolves, who needed help.

Even though he hadn't wanted to love anyone for fear of losing them, he'd never been sorry that he'd stepped back into the stream of life. Now that the chance of a *full* life—a family—hovered just out of reach, he had to do everything in his power to live, to take a chance and make sure that she did, too. He wouldn't leave Tracey to live in fear anymore either.

Tav knew that nothing would change overnight. He could live with that.

* * * *

Tracey shivered with a slight wariness when Tav walked into the yard carrying his axe and his toolbox the next morning before Ashley left for school. It was a very large toolbox, but he carried it as if it were empty.

Sitting on the porch with her back to the wall beside the front door enjoying her morning coffee, she couldn't believe the zing that went through her body at the sight of her handsome neighbor. She didn't understand what he wanted or why he kept coming back but she couldn't deny that he had an effect on her. She'd felt it since first laying eyes upon him.

While his presence still made her a bit uneasy, he brought with him a feeling of calm and security that she hadn't felt since she was a girl still living with her parents. Tracey wanted to feel whole again. She'd see what he wanted, Tracey decided. Maybe she'd let him stay around a bit – as long as he behaved himself.

Tav walked to the wide porch and set his toolbox down on the ground in front of it. He lowered himself to the porch steps and leaned over to pat her sock-covered foot.

"Morning Tracey," he smiled. "Is that coffee I smell?" he asked wistfully.

She had every intention of demanding that he tell her why he was there and then telling him to leave and get his own coffee.

"Would you like a cup?" she heard herself ask. *Damn that decent upbringing and doubly decent parents!*

"I really and truly would," he said softly with just the hint of a smile.

Disgusted with herself, she rose and went inside to get it. *I do NOT want him here! I certainly do not! He'll change – I know he will. All men do.*

Tracey could kick herself for her thoughts. *Sorry Daddy, and to my big brother Jimbo!* There were some good men in the world still, like her father and older brother, Jim, but she knew that men could change their spots in the blink of an eye. She hated that her trust of men was nearly non-existent, but the years with her ex had taught her that she really couldn't rely on anyone but herself in life. While she loved her family, she couldn't put her burdens upon them, nor put their lives in danger. Though she knew they'd help her, her ex would use them against her; she knew he would if given the chance. She just couldn't accept that as an option, knowing they'd understand why she didn't visit or call them often.

Automatically, she added milk to a large mug and poured the hot coffee into it. As she turned to carry it outside, she stopped. *I don't know how he likes his coffee. I don't drink my coffee this way. Why'd I do that?*

Tracey took a deep breath and walked out to the porch with the mug. Gingerly, she set it between them and nudged it toward him. After she'd seated herself back against the door, he reached out and took the mug.

"This is perfect. How'd you know how I like it?" he grinned at her. He seemed so pleased that it made her a little uncomfortable.

Looking away, she shrugged and mumbled, "You drink a lot of milk."

"Good coffee," he nodded, looking off into the yard.

Neither spoke for some time, just enjoying the quiet morning. It was a companionable silence, but soon, Tracey heard Ashley stirring. When she heard the toilet flush, she went in and gave Ashley a hug.

Ashley was such a contradiction sometimes. She was so independent that she bounced out of bed and pulled her clothes on right away. The little girl always liked to choose her own breakfast and make it if it needed making. But as independent as she seemed, if she didn't get a hug and a kiss from her Mama first thing though, her day was shot.

As a mother, Tracey knew that, because of moving so much and trying to stay one-step ahead of their father, Ashley had more worries than most children her age. If a hug was all it took to reassure her little girl and help her start the day feeling loved and secure, Tracey was more than glad to provide one.

Ashley had grabbed her breakfast muffin and poured a glass of milk when Tracey stopped her. They liked to sit on the porch and chat while Ashley ate and before she left for her bus. Tracey couldn't take her and leave the boys alone, even for a short period of time.

It was agony for her. She usually walked Ashley as far as she could go and still keep an eye on the house. Unless the boys were with her, Tracey stood in the road every morning listening until she heard the bus drive away.

At six, Jacob was old enough now to attend kindergarten for half the day and maybe, if they stayed, Tracey would enroll him after Christmas. Right now, it was hard enough to be parted from Ashley all day – academically she knew her daughter was fine, but she still worried.

"Ashley?" Tracey stopped her. "You remember Tavist Darke?" Ashley nodded. "He's out on the porch drinking a cup of coffee." Tracey waited, unsure of how Ashley would react.

Tracey couldn't read anything in her child's nearly black eyes. Finally, Ashley turned and picked up a second muffin.

"Are you going to have one, Mama?" she asked.

"Okay," Tracey answered, confused. She grabbed a muffin and followed her daughter.

She watched Ashley closely as the girl went through the door and walked up to the man seated on the edge of the porch. She stopped just a little closer than arm's length away. Tracey couldn't believe how much trust she was showing this man. Ashley never got within grabbing distance of a man. Not ever.

"Would you like a muffin, Tav?" she asked, holding it out.

"Doggone right I would!" he grinned. He held his palm out so that she could set the muffin in the middle of it.

He waited, Tracey noticed, for the child to move away before he closed his hand around the little cake.

"Did you sleep okay, Ashley?" Mostly, she just wanted to start a conversation before any awkward tension could build up.

"Umm," she hesitated, "At first I didn't, but then I did."

Tav smiled. He still didn't say anything. Tracey, finding his continued silence a bit unsettling, opened her mouth to ask him why he'd come this morning lugging his giant toolbox when Ashley spoke up.

"Tav?" He turned more fully to look at her. She was seated next to her mother near the door. "How come you don't have any kids?" she asked.

"Ashley!" Tracey gasped. She couldn't believe her daughter would ask such a personal question, especially of a near-stranger, and a man at that.

"It's okay, Tracey," he calmed her softly, putting his muffin and his coffee down beside him. Looking at Ashley, he said, "I had a little boy."

Tracey watched, horrified as the big man's eyes became shiny with tears. He held them back somehow. She couldn't believe the emotion this man showed, especially in front of two people he barely knew. In all her life, Tracey had never seen a grown man shed a tear, or even get choked up. It just drew her to him still more.

"He'd be your age now, in the third grade." He swallowed noticeably. "He and his mother were killed by a drunk driver seven years ago. Tate was still a baby."

Nobody moved for several seconds. Then Ashley launched herself at Tav, tears running down her little face.

"I'm so sorry, Tav!" she sobbed. "I'm so sorry God took your family away."

He wrapped his arms around her waist and she wrapped her arms around his head.

Tracey watched the two with tears running down her own face. *I need a box of tissue and a box of chocolate, S.T.A.T.!*

She heard him mumble something and scooted a little nearer.

"I still miss them, Ashley, but maybe…" Tracey could barely hear what Tav was saying, muffled by Ashley's body. The child leaned back and put her hands on either side of his face.

He spoke again, his voice choked with unshed tears. "Maybe God decided somebody else needed me to love them more. I know He's looking after Tate and his Mommy now."

Ashley took a deep, shuddering breath and nodded. When the child went in to wash her face, brush her teeth and gather her books, Tracey stood.

Tav was sitting on the edge of the porch looking off into the trees, lost in his thoughts. Carefully, she approached him and squatted behind him, placing her hand on his shoulder.

"I'm sorry, Tavist," she whispered.

He laid his cheek on the hand that gripped his shoulder. She thought she felt a little moisture there but she couldn't be sure. To lose a child…it was something she just couldn't even think about without dying a little inside. Her heart ached for Tavist and all he had endured. Emotions welled within her that she couldn't dwell on. Tavist Darke was wreaking havoc on her senses.

The moment was broken when Ashley came out, planted her tiny hands on slim hips and demanded, "Okay, which one of you is gonna be walking me to the bus stop?"

* * * *

Tav laughed. "I guess that's me, huh?" He winked at Ashley. "If that's the price for having breakfast with two such pretty ladies, I'll pay up."

He quickly downed the rest of his coffee and stood. Truthfully, he needed to move a little and get his mind past the conversation the three of them just had.

He kept his focus completely on Ashley as they headed down the dirt road which would lead them to the bus stop. She slipped her hand into his and smiled shyly up at him.

"I met a wolf outside last night, Tav," she confided. "He looked big and mean but he wasn't."

He looked at her and arched a brow, but said nothing.

"Did you ever meet any wolves?" she asked him.

"All my friends are wolves, Ashley. They look big and mean but they're just silly mutts."

"Do they ever *get* mean?" she wanted to know. Her level gaze left no room for falsehoods of any kind.

"They do," he admitted solemnly.

Her eyes were round as she regarded him nervously.

"When?" she breathed.

"Whenever they find out somebody hit a little girl or her brothers or her mother."

Her grin evolved slowly as she realized his words. "I'd like to meet more of your friends, Tav," she told him finally, her dark eyes sparkling happily.

"You will," he assured her, "I promise."

As they passed the nearly invisible drive that led to his house, Tav stopped. Pointing, he told Ashley, "That's the road to my house. If you go out your back door, you can walk right up to my back door – it's a straight line."

"Okay, Tav," she dimpled up at him. "Tav?" she said hesitantly, as they resumed their journey.

"Yes, Ashley?" he responded, looking down at her.

"Did I make you sad by asking you about your little boy and his mommy?" Her little hand trembled in his but she bravely hung on.

"No, you didn't make me upset. I miss them because I loved them and they aren't here anymore. I'd miss them even if nobody ever asked. I can miss the people I love and still be okay." He hoped he said the right things. *Am I way out of my league here?*

"Do you think you could ever love any other mommy and – and kids?" she asked after a minute of quiet.

"I'm pretty sure I could, Ashley," he smiled at her.

Leaning down, he gave her a quick hug as the bus pulled to a stop. He watched her board the bus and turn and wave before the door closed. His heart felt like a wrung out dishrag.

On the way back to Tracey's house, Tav stopped at home and made a phone call to his pack leader and mentor, Mik Montgomery. Mik was the closest person Tav had to a father since his own parents had been killed when he was a young pup. He'd met Mik when the renegade werewolf, August Livingston, had attacked the older Were's daughter-in-law, Bethany, and her pups.

She'd decided to hide out in the White Mountains of New Hampshire. Determined to protect her, Tav had caught up with her there and stayed in wolf form to help her. Mik, the pups' grandfather, had shown up within days and stayed with them.

Mik Montgomery was the only Were that Tav could ever consider his Alpha. His sons, Riker, a famous actor and mate to Bethany, and Lakon a famous singer now mated to Mya, were two of his best friends. In fact they were like brothers to him. He'd stepped in to help on separate occasions when Auggie took Bethany and later when Mya was attacked, thus earning himself a place in the Montgomery family pack along with the nickname, *Underdog*.

Right now, though, he didn't need a brother, he needed a dad.

"Hi Elke, it's Tav," he said when Mik's mate answered the phone.

"Tavist!" she squealed. She made him feel so welcome. If Mik wasn't at home, he'd talk to her. "How are you, son?"

"I'm okay, I guess, Elke. Not bad at all. You okay?" Sometimes he wasn't sure what to say, though he loved talking to his surrogate mother.

"I'm fine – busy planning for my new grandbabies. Oh! Here's Mik. He wants to talk to you. I love you, son." She was gone before he could answer.

"Hey, Tav." He heard the talking-in-a-barrel sound of being placed on speakerphone. "Everything okay?"

Mik's deep, rough baritone made him feel like a pup again, safe in his family's den. He took a deep breath.

"Mik, I think I found my second mate and she's got three little kids." Elke's squeal in the background brought a smile to his face.

"More grandbabies and I don't have to wait!" she crowed.

"Elke!" Mik growled impatiently, "I'm in the middle of a conversation here, love!" Tav snickered at the squabbling couple. *You just can't end a sentence with the word "love" and sound firm, you just can't. Not even if you're badass-Mik Montgomery.*

"I'll leave," he heard Elke call out. "Tavist, you'd better let me know the very *minute* I can come and start spoiling those children. Do you hear me, young man?" Tav laughed.

"I promise, Elke. The very second."

"Three grandbabies! You're my *favorite*," she swore. "I'm going, I'm going."

Mik rumbled a growl at her, though he didn't sound all that menacing. "What's wrong, son? You didn't just call to get your mother all worked up, did you?" Tav loved when they forgot that he wasn't really their pup.

"She's a human and the kids are human. Her ex beat the shit out of all of 'em, repeatedly – except maybe the three-year-old. I'm not even sure about that."

"Where'd you say this man is now?" Mik asked, his tone carefully nonchalant.

"He's in jail, Mik. If he wasn't, he'd already be dead."

"Another human in the family, huh? There'll be a whole bunch of humans in the family. I bet you boys are drawn to human mates because of the extra wolf on my side," Mik mused aloud.

"Mik," Tav said quietly, "I don't *have* the extra wolf, remember?"

"You feel so much like my own son, boy, I just forget sometimes."

He could hear Mik's smile. Tav was grinning like a fool. Mik always knew what to say to make him feel stronger—a part of the family.

"Son, I know it's scary and it's hard since you've lost two families already. Don't forget that we're all here for you. You have a very big family pack now and we'll welcome your mate and her children. You can do this, Tav. You'll handle it all just fine." Mik really *did* know just what to say.

"Thanks, Mik. I think I'm ready to gird up again and jump back into the fray," he tried to sound flippant but he knew he probably failed.

"Hey, Tav?" Mik rumbled. "So far, you're *my* favorite, too. Don't make me come down there and teach you what you already know. You need help, you ask for it, you hear?"

"Yes, sir," Tav chuckled.

They said their good-byes and hung up the phone.

Chapter 6

When Tav got back to Tracey's house, Jacob and Christopher were out of bed. Both boys seemed especially glad to see him, so Tracey decided to invite him inside.

"Tav!" Jacob rushed up and hugged him. Quickly, he jerked back and stuck his hand out stiffly.

"Men who are very good friends hug each other sometimes, Jacob," Tav told him, standing up with him in a big, rollicking bear hug, ignoring the handshake altogether.

Not one to stand for being left out, Christopher joined in on the hugging action. Soon, the three of them were rolling around on the living room floor accompanied by loud squealing and laughing.

Finally, when Tracey began to worry about possible injuries, the three of them put their heads together and began whispering. She wasn't sure if that didn't make her even more nervous.

"Me, too, me, too?" pleaded little Christopher.

"Of course you, too!" said Jacob in exasperation. "You can hold the nails and help tie the knots."

"Nails? Is somebody going to let *me* in on the secret?" asked Tracey, archly.

"We'd like to make a swing on the giant tree out back. It's perfect. C'mon, we'll show you." Tav leaned close to talk to her, his rumbling voice caressing her ear, causing her heartbeat to take off.

The boys were chattering excitedly and she even heard Tav's voice a time or two but Tracey's attention was riveted elsewhere. Tav had placed his hand in the small of her back as they left the house.

He'd taken her hand going down the stairs and then dropped it as they'd approached the tree. He'd squeezed her shoulder lightly to emphasize a point and now he was chuckling at her.

"Wool gathering, Ms. West?" he laughed, sliding his arm around her in a hug.

Dropping his arm quickly, he stepped over to the tree and squatted. "This big root here will let Christopher step up so he can get on the swing easier and without assistance." He said, repeating the earlier statement that she'd missed.

She looked at him quizzically for a minute. "I know you have an image in your mind but all I see is a tree and a big knot on the ground.

And three crazy boys who want to make something out of nothing," she teased.

Laughing, Tav looped an arm around Tracey and kissed her forehead, turning her around all in one swift movement. "You go read one of your books and make something out of that. We'll design and build our pleasure craft and call you when it's time to launch." He gave her a little shove.

At first, Tracey was a little resentful of Tav, taking her children over like this. After watching the trio for a few minutes, however, her outlook began to change. The boys needed a man around to appreciate and admire. They only had her to pattern themselves after and, if she were honest with herself, there were times that she knew that she wasn't enough. Sometimes she needed more for herself as well. Was Tav offering her that, too? Would she accept it he did? She hadn't had the best possible experiences with men so far in her life.

How foolhardy was the idea of trusting Tavist Darke? As she stood at her kitchen window pondering the dark haired enigma tickling and tossing her boys as they created something out of nothing on that old tree, Tracey began to hope.

Whatever happened in the future, right this minute, the boys were occupied and safe, leaving Tracey with some quiet time early in the day, *before* she was too worn out to enjoy it. One should always take note of the little things, after all.

* * * *

Tracey put together six big sandwiches for lunch, knowing that the boys would be hungry later and that Tav would still be there. After sliding the covered sandwiches into her refrigerator, she watched them for a little while longer, fighting her confusion over the man. Obviously, he wasn't the monster her ex-husband was, but he was still a man. She'd like to accuse him of bullying his way in but that wasn't true either. Tracey had to be honest with herself, no matter how inconvenient the truth could be.

Tav was no bully. He wasn't pushing his way into their lives. He just tried to fit in wherever he could – making a place for himself with them. While it made her nervous, *very* nervous, she knew it wasn't altogether a bad thing.

She felt pleased that Ashley was opening up to him. Although there was nothing wrong with being cautious, Ashley's fear of men had been nearly incapacitating. Tracey had already been to the school three times to talk about her reaction to an older boy crowding her or the older male janitor shouting at a group of kids. Ashley had hidden in a little used closet for hours and caused quite a stir. Somehow, though, her little girl felt safe with this big man.

Since she wasn't getting anything done anyway, Tracey decided to run to the store while she had the chance. Grabbing her car keys, she went out the back door to ask Tav if he'd mind being alone with the boys. It was something of a risk, but she felt she could take the chance. After the emotional morning, she felt more and more like she knew him.

"Tav, can I ask you for a favor?" She called hesitantly.

He stood and Jacob took Christopher's hand and they moved back from the tools. Tav turned to Jacob and, pulling off his gloves, gave him a big smile and a thumbs-up. He strode over to Tracey.

"Name your pleasure, ma'am," he grinned. At her blank look he said, "The favor?"

"Oh," she shook her head, smiling in embarrassment. "Would you mind being here alone with the boys while I run to the store?"

His grin grew wider. Looking over his shoulder, he winked. "Only if you bring us back some chocolate milk."

She laughed. She could hear her sons chattering excitedly. Apparently boys of all ages loved chocolate milk. Tav continued walking with her to the side of the house where her car was parked.

She bent to unlock the car door and turned to the big man still next to her. She felt frozen in place as he cupped her cheek.

"Tracey? Thank you for trusting me," he murmured.

She stood unmoving as he lowered his head to hers and brushed her mouth in a feather-light kiss. When she still didn't move, he kissed the tip of her nose and turned, calling out to the boys as he rounded the back of the house to rejoin them.

She stood frozen for several minutes, shocked that he'd kissed her that way. She wasn't sure which surprised her the most – the fact that he'd kissed her or that she'd let him. It looked like Ashley wasn't the only conquest Tav had made among the West women.

With a start, she realized that she was still standing beside her car in a daze. She could hear Tav and the boys chattering and laughing in the back yard. Shaking herself both physically and mentally, Tracey opened her car door and climbed in. As Tracey drove into town, her thoughts skittered from Tav and his touches – and his lips – to the overwhelming sense of freedom she felt at that moment. It had been years since she'd been able to do anything alone.

When she'd first begun dating Jack Aschtholdt, her children's father, everything had seemed so right. He'd treated her well and Tracey's parents had approved. Even after their engagement, he'd been good to her. Then, he'd become possessive – jealous, really. He was always so sure that she couldn't be faithful to him. It had seemed romantic to a twenty-year-old engaged to be married.

Later, after the wedding, his behavior had gotten worse and worse. Tracey hadn't done anything on her own in nine years. She'd finally managed to divorce Jack after he'd been put in prison for child and spousal abuse. She believed she'd be notified if he ever got paroled but she didn't dare leave the kids with sitters – just in case. As for enjoying time to herself, that was nearly impossible with three young children to care for.

Now, out of the clear blue, she was shopping, browsing and enjoying some quiet time on her own. She felt downright giddy.

What was it about the big man that made her yearn to trust him? In fact, she *must* trust him more than she'd realized, otherwise, how could she leave her most precious sons with him? But she didn't regret it—it was amost instinctual. She'd almost had to fight to resist the man. Nope, she wouldn't worry about that now. Instead, she would enjoy her freedom while she had it and explore the situation later, when she got home.

* * * *

"How it's going to work, Jacob, is with a pulley," Tav explained. "See, the rope fits on the groove of the wheel. We'll tie this part of the rope to the swing. When you pull this rope, the wheel turns and the swing will move up. If you pull on the other one, the swing will move down."

"That's so cool!" crowed Jacob. "Baby Christopher can pull it so he can ride it whenever he wants, right?"

"Yep, that's the plan," Tav agreed. "Let's rest a minute."

"Tav, how do you know all this stuff?" asked Jacob.

"I just learned it, Jacob. But now that we're friends, I'll try to show you the stuff I learned, okay?" Tav gave the boy a quick hug.

"Where do you live, Tav?" Jacob asked.

"I live right down that path, son. Let's grab Christopher and walk over there and back. It's not far. We'll only go close enough to see the house and my studio. It's just on the other side of the house and a bit behind. I want you to know where I live in case you ever need me."

"Okay, Tav, I think that's a very good idea," Jacob agreed sagely. "Christopher! Wanna go for a walk?"

With Tav holding Christopher's left hand and Jacob holding his right, the three of them walked up the path into the woods. It was a very short walk.

"Do wild animals live in these woods?" Jacob asked in nervous awe.

Christopher let out an impish little roar. Laughing, Tav hauled him into his arms and growled into his neck.

Lifting his head, he told Jacob, "I'm the wildest animal that lives in these woods, Jacob." He looked at the boy intently as they came within sight of his house. "See how close I live?" he asked. Jacob nodded. "If you ever need something, son, if there's ever something wrong, you stand in your backyard and yell it out, okay? I'll hear you, I promise." Wide-eyed Jacob nodded. "Now, let's see who can be the scariest wild animal to come *out* of these woods!"

Jacob laughed and the three of them began to run back down the path roaring and growling.

* * * *

Tracey didn't know what to think of the sight that greeted her when she parked her car in her driveway. Her sons were chasing Tav around the yard, growling and roaring at him until he caught them. It turned out that his growl and roar sounded much more believable then theirs.

He scooped a squirming, giggling boy in each arm and walked up to her, placing them on the ground at her feet. "I believe these ferocious creatures belong to you?"

"Will chocolate milk soothe the savage beasts?" She produced a bag containing three cartons of the precious nectar. The boys squealed with glee, reaching eagerly for their treat. "How were they?" she asked as she handed them the cartons and watched them guzzle their drinks.

Tracey tried not to watch Tav too closely. Still, she couldn't help watching as he tipped his head back and swallowed a long gulp of milk. When his tongue swiped at a drop of creamy chocolate hovering on his lower lip, she forced herself to turn away.

"They were great. We had a fine time. In fact, we're all ready to hang the swing but we wanted to wait for you so we walked a little ways into the woods." At her worried frown, he went on. "I just wanted to show them where my house is. We didn't go all the way to it."

"Oh, okay." Tracey wasn't sure how she should respond, how she should feel. "Let's have lunch and then we'll hang the swing. I made the sandwiches earlier so we can just get right to it," she promised, glad to include the boys and thus have a buffer between herself and her potently male neighbor.

The lunch plan seemed to be a hit so she went to bring out the food. Tav had surprised her by telling her that he preferred to eat outside when he could. She had to agree that it was a lovely day and they should enjoy it before the weather turned cold. Needless to say, Christopher and Jacob were very pleased with the idea.

Lunch was consumed and cleaned up with rapid dispatch. It was obvious that Jacob and Christopher were anxious to try the swing.

"Tracey, did you enjoy yourself in town earlier?" Tav asked politely after taking a bite of his sandwich and a drink of his milk.

She opened her mouth to answer and Jacob interrupted. "Of course she did, didn't you see her smiling? Hurry and eat, Tav, so we can try it out!" the little boy ordered him.

Once again, she was prevented from speaking, though this time she meant to reprimand Jacob for his rudeness, but Tav, calmly and gently intervened.

"I asked your mother a question Jacob, and she was going to answer me. All good men know that it's rude to interrupt when others are talking," he said quietly. "You forgot, didn't you?" he asked with an understanding smile.

Jacob blushed profusely and dipped his head. "Um, yeah. I mean, yes. I'm sorry for interrupting, Mom."

She gave herself a little shake and answered, "Everybody forgets, Jacob. Just try your best." She turned to Tav again and shared a smile with him. "I had a great time in town earlier, Tavist. Thank you for asking me about it."

"Well, we certainly had a good time working on our little project while we were gone, didn't we boys?" He looked around at both children.

Christopher crowed and clapped his hands, squirming with excitement.

"We worked real hard, Mama," Jacob said seriously, trying hard to sit still. "Just wait till you see!"

Tav winked at Jacob and nudged him. "Jacob, I bet your mother would really like to know how our new swing is going to work."

"Oh, yes," Tracey grinned, enjoying the game. "Please, Jacob, tell me all about it." She looked at him wide-eyed and nodded her encouragement. For a moment, she'd been unsure about Tav's intervention with Jacob, but he'd handled it so smoothly and gently, she couldn't really object.

Now, she hid a smile as she listened to Jacob proudly explain how the pulley worked as Tav shimmied up the tree and looped the ropes over a thick branch. Jacob was pleased to show her the little boards that could scoot up to form a back and sides on the swing so Christopher didn't fall out the front or back. They could be taken away if you were big enough not to need them.

Finally, the deed was done and the swing hung ready for its maiden journey. There was some debate over who would get the first ride, but Tav took the first turn so that he could test the strength of the ropes. First he took a swing by himself and then held Christopher on his lap. After five minutes of swinging with the squealing toddler, Jacob climbed onto Tav's lap. When his five minutes were up, the boys insisted that Tracey sit on Tav's lap and swing.

He didn't help her at all, the rat! He just sat there grinning with his eyebrows raised.

When Jacob whispered, "He doesn't smell bad, Mom, really," her fate was sealed.

She gingerly perched on one of his knees until Tav looped an arm around her waist and pulled her firmly up. "I can't have you falling off, Love. Safety first."

Then, he dug his feet into the ground and gave the swing its push. She couldn't stop herself from giggling like a little girl. It felt so good to be snug against this man's broad chest with the wind in her hair.

The boys ran in circles, clapping with excitement. After the preordained five minutes, Tav slowed and stopped the swing.

"We'll have to do some more of that later," he rumbled into her ear, letting her off the swing. Tav's teasing and flirting unsettled her somewhat, but maybe not as much as she'd thought it would, had she given such a thing very much consideration.

The boys continued to play with the swing for another half hour before Christopher began to yawn. Tracey didn't have the chance to say a word.

"I'm gonna go in with Baby Christopher and read him a story, Mom," Jacob told her. "It's been a busy morning and I want to rest." His face turned red. "I liked hanging out with him today. I'm not done yet."

Tracey stared in awe as her six year old led his little brother into the house.

Turning to Tav, she frowned. "What just happened here?"

"I don't know," he replied, "but it was pretty cool, wasn't it?" She nodded.

"I'm just going to tiptoe in and peek. Be right back." Tracey said.

Tav grinned. "Okay."

She came out a minute later, her eyes moist with tears. "It's the sweetest thing. He's reading, "*Go Dog Go*" and Christopher's fighting to keep his little eyes open."

* * * *

"I think you should celebrate the moment by swinging," Tav told her. "I'll push."

After a moment's thought, Tracey capitulated. She spent a little time inspecting his "marvel of engineering", all the while making the appropriate sounds of admiration and appreciation, until finally, she climbed aboard. He stepped behind her and gave her a push.

Leaning against the tree, he watched her, enjoying the sight of the wind whipping through her blaze colored hair. She had a wide, joyous smile on her face. *I wish I had my sketchpad…*

"Remember when you were a kid, Tav?" She had a look of mischievous childish delight on her face. "Did you ever do this at the playground?"

"What?" he asked smiling at her. The smile vanished when she launched herself from the swing. Two stumbling steps later, she was rolling in the grass.

He shot across the yard after her, thinking she was writhing in pain. When he came to his knees on the grass beside her, he found her laughing with joy. Without a thought, he pulled her into his arms, laughing and tumbling along with her.

"Woman!" he growled. "You scared the *hell* out of me!"

Still laughing she said, "I think you probably have some hell left in you."

Looking down at her, he felt the air leave his lungs. "Do you know how beautiful you are, Tracey West?" Her wide, blue eyes were fixed on him, her pupils dilated. "You literally take my breath away," he groaned.

He reached out, stroked her hair, and gulped back a low, hungry growl. Giving in to his hunger, he covered her mouth with his. Willingly, she parted her lips, moaning softly as his tongue stroked into her mouth.

She kissed him back just as hungrily, her tongue mating with his, exploring his mouth. Suddenly, she froze. He realized that he'd moved over her just a little and his erection pressed her thigh.

Abruptly, she began to struggle frantically. Sadness warred with embarrassment—he knew what she was afraid of. "Tracey?" he edged away from her, releasing her. "Don't run away, Tracey."

He saw the wild, panicked look in her eyes but she didn't run. She backed up until she came to a tree and pressed against it.

"You – your…I wasn't trying to…" her breathing was still ragged and her voice was pitched high.

"I got hard because kissing you and holding you felt so good. Maybe kissing me felt good, too? Just a little?"

Her face turned red, but she said nothing.

"Tracey, I'm not going to pretend that I wouldn't like to make love with you someday. You understand?" She nodded. "You may never feel that way. I hope someday you do. I will never do anything you don't want me to do. Okay?"

He began to climb to his feet, holding out his hand to her. After long, indecisive seconds, she took it and let him help her to her feet.

* * * *

Brushing herself off, Tracey came to a decision. "Ashley won't be home for an hour or so and I'm sure the boys are asleep. How about I buy you a cup of coffee?" she joked, heading for the kitchen.

Obviously startled, Tav looked at her and nodded. He stayed out on the porch while she went inside to fix the coffee. After several minutes and a million deep breaths, Tracey brought Tav a steaming cup of coffee.

They sipped at their coffee for a few minutes, keeping their thoughts to themselves. After a short while, Tracey cleared her throat.

She forced herself to speak. "Tavist, you can't miss the fact that I was married before."

"Um, no, I guess that didn't escape me," he smiled slightly. "Or at least the part where you've been intimate with at least *one* man…Judging from your reaction to what happened earlier, I guess you know it wasn't a slice of heaven?" She arched a ginger colored brow at him. "Ashley and Jacob have said a few things," he confessed.

Astounded, she considered him over her coffee cup. "I guess it says something that they trust you enough to talk to you."

He nodded and shrugged saying, "I'd like to think so."

She let out a breath. "It was bad, Tavist. Some things happened that the kids don't know about – thank God."

He nodded, looking at her unblinking.

"Jack, my ex-husband, used sex as punishment. Truthfully, he used *everything* as punishment." She took a sip of her coffee.

Tav took a gulp of his, turning his head. *Wasn't his hair above his collar earlier? Can hair grow that fast?*

Shaking her head to clear those odd thoughts, Tracey went on. "I like you, Tavist." Smiling wryly, she said, "Nobody's more surprised than I am, believe me."

He looked back at her and smiled that endearing half smile of his.

"Tavist, I just don't know if I could ever be more than friends with a man again. I just wouldn't want you to expect more from me than that." There, she'd said it. She sat rigid, waiting.

He sipped his coffee again and then put the cup down, turning to her. "Can I tell you a little about how I feel, Tracey?" he asked, politely waiting for her to respond. She nodded. "Liking a woman, loving a woman, having a mate – it's about more than sex." She saw that mischievous little boy smile again, "Don't get me wrong, I've got nothing at all against sex." He winked. "But loving, liking, and mating are about caring. You want to be with that person, know they're safe, comfortable, and happy. Just sharing moments, good and bad is what I hope for – assuming things ever got that far…"

"Tavist, I don't know if I could ever get past worrying that you'd change – that someday, you'd hit me or hurt me." She felt her eyes filling. *I'm definitely going to bed early tonight. I'm emotionally exhausted. What a day!*

"One of my best friends did something to hurt his woman. That's very unusual for our kind," he began. *Our kind?* "She told me she'd worried about him doing it again. When they talked about it, he told her to try to trust him for just a few hours and then a few more." He gave her a little smile. "I was really proud of him when she told me that."

"I guess he might have something there…" she slanted a look at him. "Just…Well, I don't know, okay?"

"Fair enough. I think it's a big deal that you'd even consider being my friend." He stood and picked up a napkin that had blown away at lunch. Turning back, he looked at her for several minutes.

"What?" She asked.

"Jacob said that Sue would be visiting for a day or two next week."

"Yeah?" she wasn't sure where this was going.

"I've got tickets to a big outdoor concert next week. I'd sure like to take a friend. Will you think about it?" he asked, making it easy enough to back out.

"Tavist…" she felt her stomach drop as she stared into those beautiful gray eyes. *I could drown in those eyes. He definitely doesn't blink enough, though.*

"Think about it. Talk it over with Sue. I won't be mad if you don't go. I promise I won't even bring it up again. Just let me know if you decide to go."

He handed her the napkin he'd picked up and held his other hand out. After a minute, she took his extended hand. He raised it to his lips and kissed it, dropping it quickly.

"I'll go and meet Ashley's bus but I won't bother you anymore today," he smiled.

The poor man is probably as emotionally exhausted as I am.

* * * *

"Tav!" Ashley came running toward him and then stopped short. "Hi, Tav."

"Hi, Ashley!" He smiled. "How was school?"

"I get to dance in the school play! Aunt Sue always took me to my dance classes and now I get to dance in the play!" She was so excited she could barely walk straight.

He gave her a quick hug. "I'm so proud of you! I can't wait to see you dance. You'll have to tell me when, okay?"

She looked at him, shocked. "You'd really come, Tav?"

"Wild horses couldn't keep me away, young lady."

She grabbed his leg and gave him a tight hug. "Mom will get to come this time, too. Daddy can't stop her now, can he?" She was still bubbling over with enthusiasm.

"Nope, nobody can. She'll be there, too." It was hard to keep his voice even but he managed it. "Hey! Wait till you see what Christopher and Jacob and I did today." He grinned at her.

"What? What did you do?" He'd never seen her act so much like an eight-year-old girl.

"It's a surprise. Jacob and Christopher will tell you all about it." As soon as the words were out of his mouth, Jacob and Christopher came tearing up the dirt road.

They were only a few feet from Tracey's yard now so Tav stopped. "I'll see you guys in the morning, okay?"

Ashley hugged him quickly and ran off to meet her brothers. Their excited chattering warmed Tav as he walked back to his own house.

Although he had dozens of pictures in his mind that he wanted to sketch out, he picked up the phone. He had a very important call to make.

Grabbing a cold drink out of the refrigerator on his way by, Tav made his way into his den. This call could drag on, or become uncomfortable. Calling one of his adopted brothers could lead to any number of unanticipated events. With that in mind, he wanted to be comfortable, seated in his favorite chair. His ottoman was nearby, so he hooked a foot around it and pulled it close as he sat down. It took a few seconds to settle himself comfortably, and then he lifted the receiver and dialed.

"Hey Lake, it's Tav," he identified himself as soon as Lakon Montgomery answered.

"Underdog! How's Sweet Polly Purebred?" he crowed.

"Funny, very funny," Tav said dryly. "But that's not why I called."

"Are you going to make me guess or are you going to tell me?" Lakon continued to antagonize him.

"You saw Marc and T. Paul, huh?" he asked, hoping to cut the explanations short.

"Nope, man, Mya saw Marc, that's all. He examined her and told her that I should ask about Sweet Polly Purebred when I spoke to you. No idea why."

Tav sighed. "First, how's Mya? Any complications?"

"No, she's doing fine and so are the pups – all three of 'em. Marc and the rest of them – they all say there's no lasting damage done from the miscarriage." Lakon still grieved for his lost pup, Tav could hear it in his voice.

"Elke's all excited. Is she making Mya crazy?" Tav asked, trying to remind the other man of happier times.

"Mya's loving it. But being able to get away helps. If she were there the whole time, I think it *would* drive her crazy."

"You guys still doing those concerts outside of Atlanta next week?" Tav asked Lakon.

"Yeah, we'll be right up the road, less than an hour away. You up for company?"

"I'd actually like to come to a concert. I thought I'd bring a date." He waited. Lakon was sure to have something to say.

"A date? A *date*! My little brother's got a date!" Tav could hear Lakon's grin. "Not Myles, he's my *baby* brother. It's Tav, baby. He wants to bring a date to one of our concerts next week." Obviously, Mya had walked up and Lakon was giving her the scoop.

"Lake? Pay attention," Tav said quietly.

"Sorry, man. Does this mean what I think it does, Tav?" Lakon's voice had dropped to a quieter tone.

"Yeah. I found my mate. My second mate. Can you believe it? But she's a little skittish so she might not want to go, but I'm hoping." Tav didn't want to disappoint Lakon either.

"I'll make sure your name is at every entrance. I want to meet her. Is she Were? If not, does she know you're Were?"

"No, she's human," he grumbled, slightly distracted by this thought. "I'm not even sure I can get her to go out with me, Lake. I think spilling the family secret is a little premature," he snapped.

"Don't you take that tone with me, young man!" Lakon snapped back at him, laughing.

"I'll let you know, okay?"

"Okay, fair enough, little brother," Lakon said. "Try not to worry too much, hmm?"

"Sure, of course not," Tav sniped, but he couldn't hold back a smile.

"There's a good lad," Lakon said in a patronizing, terrible British intonation. "Later, Underdog," he snickered.

"Later," Tav agreed, grinning as he hung up the phone.

* * * *

Tav was out hunting and sniffing around his acreage when he heard a little voice.

"Tav?" Ashley called softly, "Tav the wolf?"

He turned and loped toward her house. As he came out of the trees, he found her in the same place he had the previous night.

"Hi, Tav," she smiled up at him.

He leaned down and licked her cheek. She giggled.

"Did you see the other Tav today?" she asked him. He nodded. "Did he tell you about my play?"

Tav wagged his tail and licked her face again. She hugged him tight.

"I like it here, a lot Tav. I hope we can stay here a really long time," she said into the thick fur at his neck. "The boys on the bus aren't even teasing me anymore. It would be so great not to move again."

I hope you can stay here forever, Ashley.

"I have to go to bed but I wanted to ask you something." He looked down at her. "Will you tell the other Tav that I really like the swing he made with Jacob and Christopher and thanks?"

Tav nodded and wagged his tail. He licked her chin and stood. She stood too and hugged his neck again. He watched as she turned and tiptoed back into her house. He listened until he heard her climb into her bed.

What a sweet, silly, shrewd little girl. Tav couldn't help but wonder how much she really suspected about himself and "Tav the wolf". Only time would tell. He hoped he'd be able to see her perform in the play she was so excited about.

Chapter 7

By the time the following Friday rolled around, Tracey felt like a politician waffling back and forth on her decision, convincing herself she should go or stay every other second. One minute she wanted to go with Tav and the next minute she was sure it was a disaster waiting to happen.

The dratted man showed up every morning, shared a quiet cup of coffee with her and walked Ashley to the bus stop. He reinforced the railing on the back porch and rebuilt both the front and back steps. He'd trimmed the bushes all around the house.

While he was doing all of this, he managed to look as sexy as sin and teach both boys various life lessons—lessons she agreed with and reinforced herself without even a second thought.

Every day, Tracey worked online promoting and maintaining Sue's review site and other, similar sites—enough to pay the household bills and put a few dollars away. She managed to get quite a bit of work done usually, while still keeping track of the boys and keeping them entertained. With Tavist around, however, she visited the library by herself, the grocery store, Wal-Mart, and had even gone to the hair salon for a full treatment. It was sheer heaven. The whole thing was making her crazy.

Tav and Tracey were silently drinking coffee out on the front porch Friday morning when Sue drove up. She placed a generous tray of blueberry muffins in the middle of the porch and then gave Tracey a big hug.

Turning to Tav she said, "Well, since you're practically a member of the family, I guess you'd better give me a hug, too!" She grinned up at him mischievously.

Tav grinned back at her and gave her a friendly hug, not to close and not too long. Tracey couldn't even pretend that he had eyes for anyone else. Sue winked at her as she moved away from Tav. He sat back down and turned his attention back to his coffee, eyeing the muffins Sue had brought..

"Sue, would you like to come in with me and get some coffee?" Tracey asked her. "Tavist, do you need some more?"

He shook his head no and Tracey could see him hide his smile when Sue winked at him.

"You shouldn't say stuff like that, Sue, it's not fair!" Tracey scolded her best friend when they got inside.

"Like what? Everybody loves muffins," Sue shrugged blandly, leaning nonchalantly against the counter.

"Don't be silly, Sue, you know what I meant. Telling him he's practically a member of the family. We barely know him!" Tracey snapped in a muted growl.

"I wasn't putting him on the spot, Tracey, and you know it. The kids love him. They're always talking about him every time I call here. It's been "Tav this and Tav that. If you were honest, you'd admit you're halfway to loving him yourself." Sue never held anything back.

Just this once, Tracey wished she would. There was nothing she could say so she huffed and turned her back to Sue, pouring her a cup of coffee.

"So?" Sue asked.

"So…What?" Tracey responded. She wasn't making any of this easy for the traitor, whether she knew what Sue meant or not.

"Did you tell him you're going to go to the concert?"

"I don't even know what concert and where…" Tracey hedged.

"Don't be a ninny, Tracey. Does it matter where, who or even what the performers are? It could be a pack of performing poodles. You know you want to go! Now quit fooling around and tell him you're going so we can go shopping. Come on!"

Tracey laughed. She couldn't help herself. Sue always cut right to the heart of the problem. Or at least whatever she thought was the problem. Most of the time, Tracey ended up agreeing with her anyway. Why not now?

"Fine!" Tracey pretended to snap. "Walk Ashley to the bus stop!"

When Tracey and Sue returned to the front porch with coffee in hand, Ashley was sitting beside Tav, chatting.

When it was time for Ashley to go to the bus stop, Sue bounced up and said, "Stay and enjoy your coffee, Tav. I'll walk with Ashley this morning."

When they were out of sight, Tracey anxiously moved over to sit by him. He turned and smiled at her, then turned back to watch the trees stirring in the gentle breeze.

"Tavist?" She was very nervous. When he turned back to her and smiled again, she continued. "Can I still come out with you tonight?"

He smiled. "Of course you can."

"I mean, it isn't too late?"

"No Tracey, it'll never be too late." He leaned over and kissed her cheek.

"Tavist, what kind of a concert is it?" Tracey asked him.

"It's not that big a deal, Tracey. Some friends of mine are playing and singing for some charity or another. Unity of some kind if I know them." He was trying to put her at ease she could tell.

Sue fairly skipped into the yard, letting Tav know that she was already aware that Tracey would be going out with him.

"We're going shopping, right?" Sue asked, rubbing her hands together.

"It wouldn't matter if I said you could just wear jeans, would it?" Tav asked.

"Nope," said Sue complacently.

"Even if I said Tracey's already beautiful and …"

Sue cut him off. "Forget it, bud. I don't make the rules. You're going out on a date and she has to buy a new outfit. End of discussion."

Tracey just watched Sue at work. She was always good for a laugh.

"Okay," Tav sighed. "These are just friends of mine – well they're my family, really. Still, it *is* outdoors. Don't forget that."

"What are *you* wearing, Tav?" Sue asked him innocently. He groaned.

Tracey had to hide her face so he couldn't see her smile.

"I'll wear dark colored jeans, nice boots and a clean…" Tracey saw Sue's eyes narrow dangerously, "…a light colored shirt that is *not* a tee shirt," he sighed. Tavist Darke was nobody's fool. "Can I use your phone?" he asked.

"Sure," said Tracey.

She and Sue went into the kitchen while Tav made his call in the livingroom. Tracey tried not to eavesdrop. She tried a little, anyway. Sue didn't bother pretending, pouring herself another cup of coffee and moving near the door.

"Hey there songbird!" she heard him say to whomever answered the phone. "How're you feeling? How're the pups?"

There was silence for a second.

"Yeah, she said she'd come. Where's that old road-dog you married?"

Tracey could hear the smile in Tav's voice. It made her feel special that he'd told his friends – his family – that he'd asked her to go to their concert. Now he was calling them to tell them she'd agreed to go. This was possibly a bit bigger than she'd thought. She was glad she'd accepted. Sue was beaming at her. *At least I'm not the only eavesdropper here.*

"Hey!" The old "road-dog" must've come to the phone. "Yeah we'll be there. Seven, right? I'll see if she wants to eat with you guys. Do me a favor…"

Tracey and Sue could hear him chuckling into the phone.

"Listen you mangy mutt, if you show your – if you embarrass me, I'm telling the old man. You'll be one hurtin' curr, buddy. I'm his current favorite you know."

He sure makes a lot of dog references…

"Yeah, I told her it was outside. How come you didn't tell me they had to shop? You know I haven't been out on a date in a decade."

Tav laughed again. "Just don't get me on her bad list before I get on her good list, all right?"

Silence again. "Yancey will meet us at the entrance? I always wondered what he did while you guys were up there belting out the tunes. See you tonight."

* * * *

The drive wasn't terribly long, but it would be more than twenty minutes. Tav settled Tracey into the passenger seat and hurried to take the wheel. He'd rented a nice roomy, late model automobile for this date, so he knew she'd be comfortable enough. His old pickup truck wasn't first-date material, not at all.

Tav could sense Tracey's anxiety, so he tried to put her at ease, though he was still new at this himself.

"Did I tell you how nice you look tonight?" he asked her.

She wore an embroidered denim dress that buttoned up the front. It hung just above her ankles and she'd left it unbuttoned from the hem to the knee. He thought it looked very sexy on her.

"You look nice yourself, Tavist," she told him shyly.

He reached over and squeezed her hand. "Thank you, Tracey. I was a little nervous." She looked at him in surprise. "It's been about ten years since I've been on a date."

"I guess we've got that in common then." she smiled.

"Maybe we have other things in common, too" he grinned.

* * * *

There was a man at the gate that looked vaguely familiar to Tracey, although she was certain she'd never met him before. He was obviously looking for someone. The crowd was much bigger than she'd realized and she didn't think they'd get close enough to really see the performers. This was *not* the outdoor bluegrass-type gathering she'd expected.

She had no idea who was performing tonight. She hadn't paid attention to such things as concerts in a long time. There was something of a list since this was a charity concert that took place over a few days.

To Tracey's surprise, she noticed the names of Lakon and Mya Montgomery, and Myles Brooks-Montgomery posted around. Looking at the elaborate marquis, she realized it had been there all along and she hadn't noticed. Now she was *really* impressed. Tav had relatives that played and sang with the Montgomerys? Perhaps it was the opening band? Or the closing act, as she remembered something about how the Montgomery family liked to open their own concerts. *Some* of their concerts…well, either way, this should be a great evening. Not that she hadn't expected to enjoy herself—much—but suddenly, her pleasant date was beginning to look like a real treat.

As she looked around, she was surprised when the man she'd thought looked familiar rushed up to Tav.

"Hey, cuz!" he said as he pumped Tav's hand enthusiastically. Turning to her he said, "You must be Tracey!"

When he would have hugged her, Tav reached out and stopped him. "She's shy, Yance," he said. "Tracey, this is Yancey Livingston. Yancey, Tracey West."

"Tracey, it's absolutely my pleasure," he grinned. "Let's get you guys up front before the fun starts, huh?"

She shook his hand, confused. *Up front?*

They followed Yancey while a big man wearing a jacked emblazoned with the word "SECURITY" fell into step behind them and another made a path through the crowd in front of Yancey.

Tracey noticed that a band, probably an opener, was already performing.

The man in front of Yancey took them to a patch of grass near the front of the stage that had "Tav" spray-painted in three-foot high orange letters.

"Good thing his name is so short, eh?" Yancey teased.

The other man spread out a very thick sheepskin, shook Tav's hand and left. Yancey gave Tav a hug, shook Tracey's hand and left also.

Tav helped Tracey get settled and made sure she was comfortable. They sat and watched the opening band finish and a young, muscular man holding a saxophone take his place. He walked onto the stage and lifted it to his lips. Looking in their direction, he lowered the instrument.

"All right, Underdog?" he grinned, arching a brow.

Tav waved a casual hand at him smiling and rolling his eyes. "Myles Brookes-Montgomery," he whispered. She recognized the man, slightly alarmed.

Tav pulled her against him as the saxophone music overwhelmed her. The guy was good. Was he Tav's family?

As the solo ended, Tracey saw Mya Montgomery come out on stage. *That's right, Myles Brookes-Montgomery is Mya Montgomery's brother...Lakon Montgomery's wife. Oh my...*Myles turned to Mya, smiling. Tracey continued to watch as Lakon Montgomery came out.

"Well? Is he here, Myles?" Lakon Montgomery asked anxiously. Everyone in the crowd could hear what the singer had to say, as his words boomed through the microphone clipped to his shirt.

Myles grinned and pointed. Mya's lips bloomed into a beautiful smile and squealed. Lakon grinned. Tracey could have sworn they were pointing at Tav. She looked over her shoulder, but there was no one close enough...nope, it had to be Tav.

"Hey you guys, look who came!" Lakon shouted as he strode to the edge of the stage. He spoke to the audience as if they were part of a small gathering of friends. This was Tracey's first Montgomery concert, but she could certainly understand the appeal. Not only were the Montgomerys vastly talented, they included the audience, almost on an individual level.

Tav scooted away from Tracey and stood up. "Lake, you giant asshat!" he growled to the man on the stage.

Lakon threw back his head and laughed out loud. "My little brother just called me a giant ass! Um...Asshat? What's an asshat, Underdog?" The crowd went nuts. *He's Lakon Montgomery's little brother? How does that work?*

To Tracey's absolute bemusement and horror, Lakon Montgomery, the mega-famous singer, jumped off the stage and strode right up to them.

"Hey brother, it's damned good to see you!" he murmured and grabbed Tav in a hug. There was a great deal of manly back-thumping as Tav hugged the famous singer in return.

"I'm gonna kick your ass, brother, but it's good to see you, too!" Tavist grunted, although he grinned with every word.

The microphone Lakon wore amplified every word each man said, but the two men ignored it, apparently used to it somewhat.

Turning to Tracey, Lakon said, "Tracey, thank you for taking pity on this sorry hound and giving him a reason to come see me." He gave Tracey a quick hug and turned to the stage. "Hey you guys, play something. I know Myles and Mya want to say hi." He turned to the audience. "You guys don't mind do ya? We'll keep it short..."

The place broke out in cheers. Shouts of "Hey little Brother! And, "Thanks for coming Tracey!" filled the air. The backup band managed to organize themselves and began playing the tune to a popular hit.

Holding a thumb up in approval, Lakon moved to the edge of the stage and lifted Mya down leaving Myles to jump off behind her. Once on even ground, Mya instantly launched herself into Tav's arms. There was a great deal of loud scraping and shuffling until Mya managed to turn off the microphone clipped to her blouse. Tracey noticed that, thankfully, the two men followed suit so that the meeting and greeting would be private.

"I'm so glad, Tav, so glad!" she sniffed. He grinned and kneeled in front of her, placing his ear to her abdomen.

Rising again he turned to Myles and gave him a big hug. Lakon had moved to put an arm around Tracey's shoulder. She was too shocked to mind. *Besides, is there one woman over the age of two on this planet who wouldn't want Lakon Montgomery's arm around her for even a second?*

When Tav turned from Myles and looked fixedly at Lakon, the singer dropped his arm and held both palms up. "Swear to God, man, I was just being welcoming."

Tav, Mya, and Myles all laughed and Tav made introductions.

"This is Tracey West and she is one very special lady. She has some very special kids, too. Tracey, meet Lakon Montgomery, Mya Montgomery, and Myles Brookes-Montgomery." He smiled and looked at each of them. "They're my family."

"I'm glad to meet you," Tracey said hesitantly.

"We'd better get up there, Tracey. We have this whole thing we do," laughed Lakon.

"I'm so glad you're here, Tracey. Tav needs someone." Mya said, giving Tracey a small hug. "Besides, I'm not the shortest anymore."

"Welcome, Tracey." Myles was obviously a man of few words. She liked his accent though.

The three of them climbed back up on stage and the concert resumed. The crowd loved the whole thing and another man wearing a jacket emblazoned with the word *SECURITY* moved to stand beside the fleece she and Tav sat on to watch.

"Tav!" Tracey whispered a little angrily.

"Yes, love?" he murmured in her ear, his deep sexy voice sending chills up and down her spine.

"Why didn't you tell me we were coming to see them?"

"I didn't…Well, I just don't think about how famous they are until I'm out with them somewhere. I've never been to one of their concerts."

"They're your family?" she whispered less harshly.

"They're the closest I have," he confided. "We've been through a lot together. My own parents were killed when I was – when I was little. I joined the army at seventeen. You know what happened after I got married—the car wreck. They adopted me – not legally like they adopted Myles, but they're my family."

Tracey would have liked to ask more questions, but Mya and Lakon were singing an aching love song to each other while Myles's saxophone throbbed in the air. It was beautiful, sensual, so compelling.

Tracey leaned against Tav and let him put his arms around her again. She relaxed after a while.

* * * *

Tracey had never had a better time out on a date. After the concert, she and Tav had joined Mya, Myles, Yancey and Lakon for supper in one of Atlanta's more unique restaurants. She had so much fun.

She loved Mya, found Lakon to be overwhelming, decided that Yancey was really sweet, and thought Myles was charming. The four of them accepted her immediately into their circle and treated her with affection and friendliness. It was as if they'd known her for years. In no time at all, she forgot that they were famous and relaxed into the lively discussions floating around the table.

The ride home was filled with comfortable conversation about the concert, the restaurant, and family. When they reached their road, Tracey asked Tav to park at his own house and walk her home.

"Thank you for coming out with me tonight, Tracey. Can I kiss you goodnight?" he asked, stopping at the tree where the swing hung in the moonlight. Tracey leaned up and kissed his chin.

"Please, Tavist, I'd like you to kiss me goodnight," she whispered, her belly tightening with his sexy rumble.

His arms stole around her as he gathered her against him. Pressed against his hard body, Tracey felt her heart beat out of control. As his mouth lowered to hers, she thought she'd die of anticipation.

His lips brushed hers gently and then a little more firmly. She sighed and he covered her mouth with his, nibbling at her lower lip. When she opened her mouth, his tongue found hers, caressing, slow and sensual.

His kisses were burning, probing and she gave herself up to them, gripping his shoulders. She felt his hands slide down to cup the rounded curves of her bottom, bringing her against the rigid proof of his desire for her.

When his knee came between hers, she felt the hard muscle of his thigh against her feminine mound. Someone else – someone with far fewer reservations than she had – rubbed herself against Tav's thigh and gripped him tighter.

Kissing his way down her chin and neck, Tav murmured, "Let me touch you, Tracey. I smell your beautiful arousal. I *need* to touch you."

"Tavist!" She could hear the breathless, high-pitched desperation in her voice. *Is that me?* "Yes, Tavist," she moaned.

Lost in his kiss, she was vaguely aware of him unbuttoning her dress at the top and at the knee. His mouth trailed down her neck and across her chest. His tongue dipped into the ample cleavage between her breasts and he massaged her buttocks inside her open dress.

In a bold move, he unfastened the front closure on her bra. She felt his mouth cover the peak of one breast, his tongue teasing the turgid nipple. His lips, his tongue moved over each peak and tasted the curve of each swell.

Tracey bit her lip and moaned, arching her back as she clutched at Tav's solid shoulders, forcing his mouth closer and harder against her bare breast.

Anchored firmly in the present, she entertained no thoughts of her ex-husband when she felt Tav's nimble fingers brush against the curls covering her mound. Somehow he'd eased her panties down and off without her realizing it.

With gentle, teasing strokes, Tav grazed her moist labial lips and she found herself opening her legs further, giving him greater access. He didn't force his advantage, instead stroking the tender flesh there lightly.

She felt her hot liquid gush out over his fingers. Tav made a sound she could only call a growl of satisfaction as he began to rub her moist flesh harder. She felt one finger enter her channel while his thumb began to massage her little nub.

Tracey had been innocent when she'd married Jack and nothing he'd ever done with her had made her feel the way she was feeling now. Her head was spinning and she clutched at Tav's broad shoulders.

He wrapped an arm around her waist, pressing her breasts against his chest. His fingers pumped in and out of her, his thumb pressing and massaging her sensitive clit. When she began to mewl and shake, his mouth covered hers again, absorbing the sounds of her climax.

Afterward, Tracey rested against him, a boneless mass of jelly. She felt him lift the hand that he'd fondled her with to his mouth. Watching him, she saw him suck her cream from his fingers.

"Mmmm," he groaned. "You taste so good, love. Thank you."

"Me?" she squeaked. It took more effort to talk than she realized. "Thank me?"

She felt his rumbling laughter against her. "Yes, love. Thank you. Thank you for sharing yourself with me that way. Thank you for making me feel like a man again." He leaned down and kissed her deeply, finally burying his face in her hair.

"Oh, Tavist," she breathed. "You're all the man any woman could ever want. I don't know why you wouldn't always feel that way."

"I only want to be the man you need, Tracey West." He stepped back and buttoned the top of her dress. She didn't know what to say so she watched him in silence.

Dropping to his knees, he lifted her panties from the ground. "Mustn't litter," he sent her his mischievous half smile, stuffing the scrap of cotton and nylon into his pocket.

"Tavist!" she yelped, half embarrassed, half excited by his roguish behavior.

Holding the sides of her dress apart, he turned his head and rubbed his face in her musky mound. He nipped at her clit and she moaned. She thought she heard him say, "Mine" as he soothed the nip with his tongue. A flash of heat shot through her.

Standing again, he buttoned her dress down to her knees and slid his palm under her elbow. They walked in silence to her door.

"Sue's leaving after lunch tomorrow?" he asked her.

"Yeah, she's going on a cruise next week," Tracey told him. "She's earned a break."

"I know you'll want to visit with her as long as you can. If you're up on Sunday morning, maybe we could have coffee?" She loved how he was trying to give her some space – but not too much. He was every woman's dream come true…maybe too perfect?

Her emotions were all over the place but she didn't want to let him go. Yes, she was afraid, but she'd be stupid not to take a chance. Tavist Darke was a good man and he wanted *her*. If his patience could stand it, she'd try her best to reward him.

"I'd like that, Tavist." She put her arms around him and hugged him. "Bear with me Tavist, please?" She hoped he would know what she meant.

"I'll wait for you as long as it takes, love," he said.

Leaning down, his lips caressed hers in an excruciating sweet kiss. She felt his fingers trail up her thigh and through the curls at the apex.

"Good night, Tracey. Thank you for going with me tonight." He pulled his hand away.

She opened her door and slipped inside. As expected, Sue, the Inquisitor, was waiting for her.

"Come into my parlor, said the spider to the fly," Sue laughed evilly as Tracey closed the door behind her.

"I guess there's no way I'm getting out of this, is there?" she asked in resignation.

"Nope, no way at all," Sue verified in a matter of fact tone.

Tracey gusted a heavy sigh. "Okay," she acquiesced. "Just let me change into my jammies. You can make some popcorn."

Chapter 8

For the second day in a row, Jack noticed that the guards had migrated toward the sandwich wagon just before five in the evening. He also realized that the days were getting shorter.

An idea began to form. If he could just wait a few more weeks, it would be full dark around five o'clock. This was a pretty large crew. He knew three or four men he could trust.

The coveralls the men wore as prisoners were bright orange. They made it pretty obvious that the wearers were supposed to be locked up. Jack thought it might not be that hard to get them dirty and muddy.

Being in prison hadn't rehabilitated him although he made every effort to convince the parole board otherwise. Every single time he went before them, and it had been two times now, someone pulled out a deposition tape of his ex-wife, Tracey, and that sniveling brat, Ashley.

The board met every four months and that wasn't long enough to forget how pathetic and afraid the mother and daughter had looked. Jack wasn't waiting for a group of people to set him free. He would take his own freedom.

As an industrial mathematician, Jack was adept at analyzing a situation, finding many solutions to problems and ultimately choosing the best one. He'd take this puzzle to bed with him and before long he'd have it all worked out.

He had to keep this quiet—not an easy thing to do when a man had to depend on another for his protection. It wasn't as if Jack couldn't take care of himself. He could. Unfortunately, part of taking care of himself meant seeking protection from those bigger and more vicious than himself. It was one more sin to lay at the feet of Tracey West and the little chit she coddled and whined over. Because of her, a strong man like Jack was forced to grovel, to perform unspeakable acts just to keep himself safe from the rabble. And now, he'd have to lie and hide to keep himself safe from the man who protected him. Tracey would pay, he'd make her watch whatever punishment he visited on that little shrew, not to mention what he did to her. Oh yes, she'd pay. After all, a man had to have something to look forward to, didn't he?

That night, before lights out, Jack Aschtholdt wrote a little love note to his family. He knew they'd moved but he also knew that the good old USPS would find them—it's what they did, right? Neither rain, sleet, snow, whatever…they'd find them, Jack was sure of it.

* * * *

Tav stepped out onto his porch and inhaled deeply. What a beautiful night. He'd enjoy a good romp, he decided, so, slipping out of his light t-shirt and old, loose jeans, he quickly transformed. As he leapt lightly to the grass, the wind shifted. He heard a small noise and his heart dropped to his toenails. *Ashley. How long has she been sitting there? Oh, man, I don't know which is worse: she saw me take my clothes off* and *she saw me transform! Well, at least it was quick, maybe she won't be scarred for life…*

They stared at each other for long minutes, the little girl and the black wolf. Finally Ashley spoke.

"Are you gonna eat me *now*?" she asked him, wide-eyed.

He couldn't help it. He began to laugh. He dropped to his stomach and covered his snout with both paws. After a minute, he rolled onto his back, still laughing. Soon, Ashley was laughing with him, scratching his ribs.

"I guess that means you're not hungry yet?" She was still giggling. He was struggling not to kick his foot in dog fashion – she'd found his itchy spot.

"I can't eat you as long as you keep scratching like that," he laughed.

"What if I get tired?" she asked. He rolled upright, sitting up.

"I'll just chew off a foot or something," he chuckled. More seriously, he asked her, "You don't *really* think I'd eat you or bite you or anything do you? I wouldn't you know. I wouldn't hit you either."

She looked up into the sky for a few seconds and then turned her eyes back to him. "Sometimes I forget that I can trust you, but mostly I know."

Tav butted against her with his head and wrapped his front leg and paw around her in a hug. "I guess you have some questions about me being a wolf, huh?"

Ashley made a sound of disgust, wrinkling her nose in emphasis. "I'm not a *baby*, Tav. You're a werewolf."

He looked at her, incredulous. "*I* knew that," he managed to choke out after some inarticulate sputtering. "I'm just surprised…" he let that trail off.

"I watch TV and read books, you know. I know it's not all exactly like they have in stories. But most kids know about witches, vampires, ghosts, and werewolves." *Was she thirty years old or eight? How old was this kid again?* How would he have reacted at her age, if he'd been confronted by something so foreign?

"You're not scared?" he asked, still amazed.

"Nah. Regular people are way scarier. Wolves and dogs don't bite you without growling at you first. Even then, it's never for no reason. It's people you've got to worry about. Men. They get mad for no reason and you never know when or why."

He opened his mouth to speak when he heard Jacob calling him. Lifting his head, he listened again. The little boy sounded upset and frightened.

"Ashley, something's wrong at your house. Run toward home, I'll catch you in about one minute." He would catch her in a matter of seconds. She didn't need to see him naked.

Ashley needed no second urging. She shot to her feet and sprinted into the woods toward her home. Transforming and pulling on his clothes in record time, Tav snatched her up as soon as he reached her and ran. Less than two minutes had passed when he emerged into Tracey's backyard carrying Ashley.

"Tav!" Jacob gasped, "Mom's hurt! I called 911. She fell and there's blood." Tears were streaming down his worried pale face.

Hugging him quickly, Tav ran in and found Tracey on the floor in the kitchen. She was bleeding on the right side of her forehead. There was an overturned chair and he could see where she'd hit her head on the counter on the way down.

He knew that Jacob had called to him right away so she'd been unconscious for less than five minutes. She still had a pulse and though her breathing was shallow, she *was* breathing.

"Phone!" he shouted. "I need a telephone!"

Both older kids seemed frozen with fear. Little Christopher toddled up and pulled the phone from the wall by its cord. He handed it to Tav. He kissed the little boy, taking the phone.

First he dialed 911 again and made sure an ambulance was on the way. He dared not move Tracey as they impatiently awaited the ambulance. Hanging up on the dispatcher, he dialed another number that he knew by heart.

* * * *

Lakon Montgomery was wrapping up rehearsal when the phone on his hip rang. It had an obnoxious clanging ring that couldn't be confused with anything else except maybe an old-fashioned fire truck.

"Lake, I need a family doctor to meet me at Union General Hospital," the speaker, Tav, said without preamble.

"Is it a Were?" Lakon asked, all business as soon as he heard Tav's tone. His pregnant wife, Mya, was looking at him, worried.

"No, it's Tracey," Tav replied, a slight tremor in his voice. Lakon could tell that his adopted brother was barely holding it together. He must be there with those children, and no doubt remembering the loss of his first mate.

Covering the mouthpiece, Lakon yelled, "Yancey, call a Livingston or Montgomery doctor to meet Tav at Union General!" Moving his hand away, he told Tav, "We're not that far, I'll meet you there."

"Bring Mya, I've got three kids with me – all under ten years old." Tav sounded relieved to have back up. Lakon couldn't blame him. Children aside, he knew he'd be a wreck if something happened to Mya—anything at all.

Lakon let out a low whistle. "Three huh? I'm on it, Underdog. We're on our way."

Hanging up the phone, he turned to Mya. Myles, her twin brother, had walked up when he'd heard Lakon call out to his manager, their cousin, Yancey Livingston.

"What's up with Tav?" Myles asked. He slipped an arm around his pregnant sister and gave her a little hug.

"Tracey's hurt. He's got her three young kids with him. Want to tag along?"

They were all close to Tav, but Lakon would have asked his brother-in-law anyway. He had fences to mend in his relationship with Myles. It had been more than a year since Lakon and Mya had separated and gotten back together, but that wasn't long enough for Myles to forgive.

"Sure, why not?" Myles agreed.

Lakon released a breath. Any time spent together would be one step closer to true reconciliation. He had too much respect for both Myles and Mya to leave things as they were.

He clapped Myles on the shoulder and led his wife and her brother out the door. They'd get through this, and help Tav get through it, too. They were a family, after all.

* * * *

Tav was never so glad to see anybody in his entire life, as he was to see Lakon when the other Were arrived at the hospital. Well, he was damned glad to see Mya, too. The kids were scared to death.

The doctor seemed a little put out to have been called south urgently to meet them. As always, the sea of chaos parted when Lakon arrived. Thankfully, that was only a few minutes after Tav, the kids, and the ambulance carrying Tracey had pulled in. The doctor who'd met the ambulance dropped his eyes and his attitude the minute Lakon walked up to the small group.

The first thing Lakon did was to grab Tav in a fraternal hug. "I'm here for you, brother," he said. Tav saw the doctor's eyes widen but the man kept them lowered and his thoughts to himself.

Christopher calmed down immediately when Mya took him into her arms. She seated herself in the private waiting room that they'd been shown to. The doctor rushed back in to treat Tracey and Tav turned to introduce Ashley and Jacob to the newcomers.

"This is Lakon and Mya Montgomery and Mya's brother Myles. His whole name is Myles Brooks-Montgomery. I'm sure you can just call him Myles," Tav told the children. "The big guy here is Jacob and the squirt is Christopher. This beautiful young lady is Ashley."

"Ashley," he heard Myles echo under his breath, inhaling deeply.

Nervously, Jacob inched forward and shook Lakon and Myles's hand. Quickly, he settled in beside Mya again. Ashley looked at Lakon and Myles and tugged at Tav. He leaned down so she could whisper in his ear.

"Are they like you, Tav?" she asked, peeking out at the three adults. All of them had seated themselves so they wouldn't seem as intimidating.

"Mya's like you," Tav whispered back. "Lakon is like me. Myles is – Myles is kind of in the middle. He can't turn into a wolf, but he can have wolf...*things*, like long teeth and such."

Ashley considered this new information before asking, "They don't hit, though, right? Even if Myles is in the middle, he won't hit me, right?" She obviously needed clarification.

Tav heard Myles shoot to his feet and stalk into the little bathroom situated in the corner of the room, turning the water on noisily. Since he'd been changed last year during treatments and transfusions used to eliminate his Hemophilia, Myles was equally werewolf and human and was obviously upset that the little girl should need to worry about being hit, although Tav sensed there was more to it than that. He hadn't missed the deep breaths Myles had been taking or the fact that he'd kept his distance. He hadn't even shaken Tav's hand yet.

"No, Ashley, they don't hit. Neither Lakon nor Myles would ever want to hit you." He reassured her.

Shyly, Ashley nodded then slipped into the chair on the other side of Mya. While Mya soothed and comforted the kids, Tav drew Lakon over near the bathroom. Myles came out and shook his hand.

"All right, Underdog?" Myles queried, hugging the other man briefly.

"Maybe I should be asking you that?" Tav countered, keeping his voice low.

Myles and Tav were the same height at five feet and eleven inches. Lakon was six feet, two inches tall. The three of them found chairs so that they could equal out the height differences.

"What's up with the hitting?" Myles growled softly.

"What's up with the inhaling?" Tav growled back, an edge to his voice.

"You first," Lakon told Myles, "Then you." He nodded at Tav.

Myles glared at him and then shrugged. "That beautiful, tiny little girl is my mate."

"What?" Tav barked shooting to his feet. Four sets of nervous human eyes fixed on him.

"Sit down!" gritted Lakon to Tav in an edge whisper. Still talking quietly he asked his brother in law, "What the fuck do you mean, Myles?"

"I enunciated clearly, Lake. She's my mate." To Tav he said, "I know she might as well be your kid, Tav. You don't honestly think I'd do anything about it now, do you?"

Tav slumped against the wall, exhaling gustily. "Shit, man, I'm sorry," Tav sighed. "It's a shock, is all. Been a hell of a day."

"Me, too, baby brother," Lakon put a hand on Myles's shoulder and squeezed. After a pause, Myles nodded. "It's going to be pure hell waiting for her to grow up," Lakon sighed.

"Yeah," Myles agreed.

All three knew that a werewolf didn't choose his mate as much as she just was. Somehow one soul out in the world waited for him to find her. So often, a male werewolf thought he'd never find his mate. Some never did.

It would be nothing short of torture for Myles to know that Ashley was out there growing up and he had to stay away. He could spend a little time with her now and then, but she'd date, get crushes, go to the prom and he would have to stand back and watch. The other fear was that something could happen to her. Tav could address that, at least.

"Don't worry, man, you know I'm going to keep her safe," he promised Myles. It was the least he could do.

"Yeah, I know." Myles took a deep breath and let it out. "So tell me about the hitting," Myles insisted.

"Maybe we should go out into the hall for this," Tav said, knowing it was going to be even uglier that the other two men thought.

Lakon couldn't stand the idea of anyone hurting kids, especially after a rogue Were had kidnapped his nephew and abused him. It didn't help that that same Were had also attacked Mya and killed his unborn pup.

Myles and Mya had been abused as children, too, especially Mya. That reality had shaped two decades of their lives. Now, finding out that Ashley was Myles's mate just added to the drama. *I can't imagine what could make this worse –please, God, don't tell me…*

When nobody moved, Tav decided he'd just spit it out. The others wouldn't get too carried away here in front of Mya and the kids, he was sure. Pretty sure…

"Tracey was badly abused by her ex. So were the pups. Especially Ashley. Bad enough that he's in jail right now." Tav braced himself.

Lakon got up and went into the hall. Myles turned without a word and went back into the bathroom, turning the water on again. Tav could hear the low snarls of both men. He hoped nobody else could.

* * * *

The doctor hesitantly made his way back into the waiting room an hour later. On some level, Tav could appreciate the poor man's predicament. He'd found himself called in to treat a patient at the behest of his pack's co-Alpha. It was an honor of sorts, really, but fraught with danger as well. What if something had gone wrong. But there was more.

Just when he thought he knew what he was about, he was surrounded by three Alphas, two of whom were Montgomery Alphas – well really all three were Montgomerys, weren't they? Tav, as acknowledged brother to Lakon and Riker and son claimed by Mik, was considered a Montgomery just as if he'd been born to the pack. Being addressed or called on by the pack Alpha was a big deal. Add to that, their reputation was definitely "take no prisoners".

The only thing the pack knew was that the last time Lakon, Myles, and Tav had been together, three werewolves had died. The only Were that hadn't died was in a Montgomery/Livingson family jail. He was only too quick to warn any who would listen of the dangers of crossing a Montgomery Alpha.

"Mr. Darke?" the doctor squeaked. "We should go out in the hall, sir."

Tav had been carrying a fussy Christopher in his arms and he put him down on a folded sheet on the floor when the doctor walked in. Mya was sitting next to Jacob, trying to get him to color with her. Ashley had been sitting, chatting with Myles when the doctor came in.

"Myles?" he heard her whisper.

"Yes, Ashley?" Myles lowered his head to hers.

"You tell me what the doctor says, okay?" When he didn't answer, she gave him a narrow look. "I know you can hear as good as Tav."

Myles looked at Tav who arched a brow and shrugged. If Ashley was truly Myles's mate, she had every right to ask this of him. It was up to him to decide how to proceed. Tav trusted Myles's judgment. The younger man would be a fool not to take this opportunity to earn Ashley's trust.

74

"If you want me to do that, Ashley, I will. I want you to know that I'll always be honest with you. Do you trust me?" Myles was no fool.

"I want to trust you, Myles. Can I?"

Lakon followed Tav into the hallway.

"Mr. Darke, your mate is suffering from a severe concussion," the doctor said nervously.

"What, exactly, does that mean, Dr. …I'm sorry, but I didn't get your name."

"Russell Montgomery, sir, I've called in Dr. Yvonne Livingston a family neurologist from Atlanta, she'll consult on this. Sir, we'll have to monitor her closely – of course. If we can keep the swelling down…" The doctor took a deep breath. "Honestly, we'll know more in a few hours." The doctor turned and left before anyone could speak.

"Looks like we're gonna be here a while, Underdog." Lakon put his arm around Tav in a show of support. "Let me take Jacob and we'll go get something to eat. I'm sure that's what's wrong with the little guy, too."

"Yeah," he breathed. "I'm sure you're right, Lake. I don't think they've eaten yet. If Jacob wants to go, that's fine." Tav was fighting panic. He'd take all the help he could get. Memories of losing his wife, Kylie, and their young son, Tate, were rushing back and he could barely hold back his fear.

When Tav wandered into the waiting room again, he saw Myles walk out with Lakon and Jacob. Ashley ran up to him and hugged him.

"Tav? Myles says Mama's got a 'cussion!" Her grip tightened as she spoke, watching her brother, along with Myles and Lakon, leave the hospital. "He says they're trying to help her and we have to wait. We don't know if she's going to be okay, do we?" Her dark brown eyes were moist and she trembled with the effort of being strong.

"No, sweetheart, we really don't. We have to hope and pray and stick together."

"Okay, Tav. Promise you'll stay with us?"

Tav lifted Ashley into his arms and hugged her tightly. "Nobody could make me leave you, Ashley. I love you guys and I'm not going anywhere."

She hugged him back equally as tightly. Setting her sneaker-clad feet back on the floor, he lowered himself into a nearby chair. Ashley sat down beside him.

"I like Myles, Tav," she whispered to him after a minute. "He makes me feel safe."

"I'm glad, Ashley. I know he likes you, too. You'll always be safe with him. Myles won't ever let anyone hurt you." He looked over her head and made eye contact with Myles who'd returned carrying his saxophone case.

Myles nodded a "thank-you" to Tav. "Hey, little Princess," he turned to her. "Want to hear some pretty music?"

Tav leaned back, closing his eyes as he listened to Myles play his saxophone. The hours passed with agonizing sluggishness. They ate the food that Lakon brought back which seemed to settle Christopher down considerably.

Mya and Lakon were singing the closing words to "Muskrat Love" when Dr. Yvonne Livingston poked her head in the door. Christopher had fallen asleep and Jacob was giving up the fight to stay awake.

* * * *

"Mr. Darke? Can you come out here, sir?" Ashley looked across to Tav from her position near Myles.

Tav nodded at Ashley who got up and sat down closer to Myles.

"Mr. Darke, your mate is showing signs of regaining consciousness. She is sleeping normally now." When he would have spoken, the doctor held up her hand. "I want you to understand, she'll probably be just fine."

"Just tell me what's happening now and as much as you can about what we should expect," Tav insisted.

"In layman's terms, her brain has gone to sleep, much like it does at night, only it's going to take it a few more days or even a week or so to wake up completely. She'll have a memory gap of before the injury – probably just a few hours. We won't know how long her recovery will take. I'll have a better prognosis after watching her a few days."

"So she's not going to die?" Tav asked. Until that minute, he hadn't realized how frightened he really was.

"I have every reason to expect a recovery," the doctor answered.

"A complete recovery, doctor?" It was time to address his other fears now.

"It could take a long time but she should regain long-term memories, motor skills, speech, all of that. Most of it will be reasonably normal before we release her. Like I said, we'll have to wait and see about a lot of this."

"What about…can we see her?" Tav knew he needed the reassurance. He was sure the kids needed it, too.

"I noticed that the little boys were sleeping. Why not bring the little girl and come on back. Just caution her that she has to be…" The doctor's mouth curved in a smile when Ashley came through the door. "I thought…"

"Myles told me," Ashley supplied. "He's my earpiece," she informed them smugly. Myles stood behind her grinning sheepishly.

"Let's go then," smiled the doctor. "I'm going to ask you to wait outside, Mr. Montgomery." Myles nodded.

Tav swung Ashley into his arms as he moved into the room where Tracey was. She was so pale, but she'd never looked more beautiful to him. Ashley gripped him tightly, clinging to him. He was sure she too was moved by the contrast of her mother's fiery red hair and her white face with the oxygen tubes and IVs crisscrossing over her.

Tav gingerly lowered Ashley to kiss her mother's face and then carefully, he kissed her as well. At the doctor's urging, they left the room. Although they were assured that Tracey had regained consciousness, she never stirred or opened her eyes. Tav tried to cling to the comfort of the doctor's expertise but it was difficult. Ashley seemed to be having as much trouble as he was keeping the faith.

"Mama didn't look too good, Myles," Ashley told him in a shaky voice.

Myles squatted in front of her and pulled her into his embrace. "Don't worry, Princess. She's alive and the doctor thinks she'll get better. We'll just have to help her, okay?"

"Okay," she agreed, sniffing, trying hard to keep the tears at bay. "It's good she's not bleeding, right?"

"Very good," Myles agreed.

Tav shuddered, catching Myles' eye. He'd never banish from his mind the image of Tracey lying on the floor, pale and covered in blood. He didn't love seeing her so small and still, with tubes coming and going, but at least she was alive and on the mend.

"Beautiful," he murmured. "She's beautiful."

Ashley's little hand slipped into his and squeezed. Obviously, she agreed.

* * * *

They stayed in a hotel near the hospital for the next few nights. Tracey was somewhat improved by the next day and Dr. Livingston let Tav bring the boys back to see her. Ashley had school and Myles dutifully drove her to the front steps, watching until she went inside and then meeting her in the same spot in the afternoon. On the first day, he'd gone in to speak with the principal, something that had caused quite a stir as it turned out.

"It's not my fault they're jammed with ruddy plonkers who got nothing to do but ponce about all day," Myles had complained. "Of course I had to stir it up a bit, didn't I?"

Tav had been at odds with the local pack leader and Myles's showing up at the school and scaring the office staff hadn't helped much. Not to mention the fact that any other Were within fifteen feet of him knew who his mate was when Ashley was nearby. Tav didn't like her chances of getting a date if she went to high school in this town. On the other hand, it would make his job as her step father a great deal easier.

Lakon had insisted on going with Mya to say hello later in the day and gave her a kiss on her forehead. Tracey didn't realize until later when she fell asleep and woke up again that a celebrity had seen her in a state of relative undress and looking her worst. She'd finally given up on embarrassment since she was still pretty confused about what and who should be embarrassing to her.

On the third day after her accident, Tav entered her hospital room to find her crying and slapping at a stuffed doll with a big smile, a button-down vest and shoes that tied. Myles, who had been behind him with Ashley and Jacob, wisely suggested they get their mother a soda from the machine.

"What's wrong love?" he asked calmly, hoping his voice was soothing to her. He took the cheerful little doll from her, rescuing it and placing it on the bedside table.

Upon seeing Tav, Tracey began to sob harder. He gathered her in his arms, stroking her hair and making nonsense noises until finally, she was no longer crying so heavily.

Breath still hitching she tried to answer him. "Shoes – tied – can't," she gasped. "Buttons! Why can't I…" she began to cry again.

"Shhh," he crooned. "You scrambled your brains a little, Tracey," he pulled back and tilted her chin up. "You can't expect everything to fall right back into place. C'mon. Take it slow. Quit rushing."

"But…my babies!" she wailed. "I have to take care of them."

"I know, I know, love. But you don't have to do it alone." He murmured, kissing her forehead. "They miss you, too. You know you won't do them any good if you push yourself too hard." He looked at her sternly. "Will you?" he demanded.

She sniffed. "No, I guess not," she agreed.

"We need you," he assured her, "we *all* need you. But we'll get by somehow until you're better. Just give yourself a break, okay? Let us help."

"I guess I'll have to, won't I?" she responded gracelessly.

"I guess you will," he affirmed, giving her a squeeze.

A minute later, she had calmed down and he'd helped her was her face, much to her disgruntlement, though before she could complain, Myles brought the kids in.

Tracey had been in the hospital for just over a week when the doctor told Tav that he could take her home the next day. Accepting that Tav could handle the kids on his own if he was at home with Tracey and the children, Mya and Lakon went on to North Carolina.

Myles decided to go home on weekends but offered to come back during the week and help Ashley get to and from the bus stop. He'd gotten into the habit of watching her practice for the school play and taking her home afterwards. Sometimes he brought one or both of her brothers with him. Tav's little house was quite comfortable and close enough to keep an eye on things without getting in the way.

The afternoon before Tracey's discharge was a day that Myles took both boys to watch Ashley get ready for her play. Tav took that opportunity to have a serious talk with Tracey.

"Tavist," Tracey said breathlessly when he sat down, "I'm so happy to be going home. I just hate hospitals, I've spent so much time in them." He wanted to pursue that line of conversation, but it was more important just now to make her comfortable with his help. With that in mind, Tav decided he'd ask her about past hospital stays at another time.

"Tracey, you know you'll need help at home for a while." She nodded. "I'd like to help you. Would you let me?"

She looked at him for a minute. "Tavist you've been so wonderful since this crazy thing happened. Are you sure you want to be tied down any more?"

"Tracey, I'd like to be tied down to you much more. But for now, I'll settle for helping you through this. Don't feel bad if you'd like me to call your parents or Sue, though." He crossed his fingers, mentally, hoping against hope that she'd give him the nod.

She held out a hand to him and he rose from his chair, easing himself down beside her on the bed next to her hip. "I think all of us would like you to stay, Tavist, if you will."

He brushed her forehead with his lips and took a deep breath. "Before you say that for sure, there's something you should know about my heritage."

Her brow furrowed. "Tavist, if one or both of your parents were a different race, well, that doesn't matter to me."

He arched a brow at her. "And what if they were a different species?"

* * * *

Tracey tried to figure out what he meant. She decided to be flippant.

"I don't much care for cats, Tavist. I'm more of a dog person." He smiled that half smile that took her breath away every single time.

"My parents were lupine. Werewolves. I'm a werewolf, Tracey."

He looked sincere. He looked like he believed what he was saying. Tracey yawned.

"Werewolf? You sure?" She yawned again. "You're not crazy are you?" She didn't know what he was going on about, but she decided to play along. She wanted him to know how much she really appreciated what he'd done for her and if this was some kind of a trust-test, she'd go with it, odd though it was.

"No, Tracey, I'm not crazy." Tav smiled at her.

Dr. Livingston came in just then and picked up her chart. "How're you feeling today, Tracey?" Tav moved so the doctor could aim a flashlight into her eyes and look.

"I'm glad I'm going home." She struggled not to yawn. "Dr. Livingston, how well do you know Tav?"

"Pretty well now." She turned to look at Tav who shrugged. "I know his family very well."

"Is he crazy? Delusional?" Tracey fought to keep her eyes open. "He says he's a werewolf."

"Nope. He's as sane as I am. He *is* a werewolf. You, however, have had quite a bump on the head. You'd better try to catch a nap before those boisterous pups of yours come to say goodnight," the doctor said matter-of-factly, flicking the flashlight off.

Tracey turned her watery eyes toward the door and watched the doctor leave. "Well, she says you're sane. That's all I care about."

She felt her eyes drifting shut. The last thing she saw before she closed her eyes was Tav's sexy half smile.

Chapter 9

Tav was getting into a routine of sorts by Tracey's second week home from the hospital. He'd followed doctor's orders for her and insisted that she do the same. There were times when he was positive that she would mutiny.

One day, he'd put both boys down for a nap after an especially busy morning and went into the master bedroom to check on Tracey. He almost lost his composure completely when he found her standing on her tiptoes on a chair in the closet.

"Woman!" he growled snatching her off of it. "I ought to turn you over my knee and spank your round little bottom!"

"You'll do no such thing!" she shrieked. "Put me down you big baboon!"

Tav tumbled her to the bed face down and pulled up the long tee shirt she wore jerking her panties down. He drew back his hand but he knew he'd never hit her. Presented with such a lovely, enticing target, however, he had to act. Reverently, he smoothed both hands over the rounded globes and leaned down and nipped at the left side pulling the panties off.

When she yelped, he licked it and nipped at the other side, lathing it with his tongue. He nipped and kissed both curvaceous cheeks leaving a darkening love bite on one side.

"Tavist!" she groaned, "Oh Tavist!" she rolled to her back holding her arms out to him.

He placed a knee beside one thigh and his other knee next to her other thigh straddling her. Taking a wrist in each hand he moved them to either side of her head, holding them there.

"Do you want to make love with me, Tracey?" he murmured, his voice low and gritty next to her ear.

"Yes, Tavist," she whispered breathlessly.

"I shouldn't let you, you know. You've been a bad girl," he admonished her sternly, trying to keep things a little bit light. He leaned down and covered her mouth with his in a passionate kiss. Raising his head a little, he murmured, "I think you've learned your lesson, don't you?"

She nodded solemnly. "I'll never stand on a chair again."

"Good girl," he breathed against her lips. "You deserve a reward."

He released her hands and lay on top of her. Wrapping both arms around her, he rolled to his back. A very feminine grin bloomed on her face.

She took his arms and pushed them above his head, tugging the tee shirt free of the jeans and up over his head. She sat astraddle his hips while she ran her fingers through the hair on his chest and leaned down to nip and lick at his nipples.

Tav could feel his erection pushing painfully against the fly of his jeans. Apparently so could Tracey. She scooted down to his thighs and began working at the button at the waist.

"Is that a gun in your pocket or are you just pleased to see me?" Tracey quoted Mae West as she tugged the zipper down, her voice low and sensual.

She found out right away that he had little use for undergarments. It didn't seem to bother her. Scooting backward, she urged the denim over his hips and down his legs.

Slowly, she crawled back between his legs and kneeled there. "Can I touch you?" she whispered.

Tav nodded. He didn't think he could speak. Tracey reached out and stroked her open fingers down the length of his erection. About the time he was sure he would die from trying to hold back, she wrapped her hand around his shaft.

He kept his hands behind his head and prayed his strength would last when she stroked his balls. He was certain he'd bite through his lip when she leaned down and touched her tongue to the slit on the hood of his cock.

"Tavist?" she whispered, looking at him with apprehension in her wide blue eyes.

"You do whatever you want, Tracey. We don't have to do anything else." He didn't know from where he found such a normal voice. He tried his best to look sincere.

"I can do whatever I want?" She turned her head slightly, narrowing her eyes as if waiting for him to qualify that statement.

"Whatever you want," he affirmed with a little nod. He closed his eyes and swallowed.

Opening his eyes, he saw a slow smile spreading across her face. "Whatever I want," she repeated with a grin.

She immediately bent down and began kissing and licking at his thighs and hips. When she moved from one leg to the other, he moaned aloud. He began groaning and clutching the comforter when she took his balls into her mouth. The air left his lungs when she nipped the head of his cock and then took it as far into her mouth as it would go.

She apparently took pity on him because she removed her mouth from his shaft and crawled up his body. "I really want you, Tavist," she whispered. "I don't think I've ever wanted this before."

She took the hem of her tee shirt and crossed her arms, pulling it over her head. "Never, ever in my whole life Tracey West, have I wanted a woman as much as I want you."

"That." Tracey said, leaning forward and dangling a rounded breast in front of his face. He took it in his mouth. "Was." She rubbed her moist woman's lips on the tip of his rigid rod. "Absolutely the right thing to say!" she gasped, lowering herself onto him slowly.

He groaned loudly. She leaned forward until he was barely in and then forced herself back down his length.

Sitting down on her knees, she raised her arms and plunged her hands into her hair, closing her eyes as she moved on him. "So good," he groaned. "So beautiful," he moaned.

He moved his hand between them and began to massage her little nub with his thumb. "Oh Tavist!" she squeaked leaning forward. He continued to massage her until he felt her sheath clench around him.

When her climax ebbed away, he asked her, "Do you want to stop, Tracey? Are you tired?"

She lifted her head and grinned at him. "Oh no, Tavist. If you're not done, neither am I. I like this."

Still joined, Tav could feel his cock pulsing inside of her tight heat. "Tracey," he said hesitantly, "Do you feel like getting a little primal?"

She arched a copper brow at him and smiled. "I'm ready to heed the call of the wild."

He pulled out of her and gently turned her over. He pulled her to the edge of the bed until her feet touched the floor. Tugging a pillow under her tummy, he kissed down her spine until she was bent at the waist on the bed with her feet on the floor.

Kneeling behind her he spread her legs and began licking at the little slit there. He drank her juices until she moaned and came around his tongue. He kissed his way back up her spine until he was standing behind her.

Holding his rod in his hand, he rubbed her dripping woman's center. She wriggled back against him and he slid into her. He held her hips and pumped once and then again.

"Yes, Tavist!" she groaned, "Oh, *yes*!" He knew that he rubbed her g-spot with every thrust.

Nature took over and he covered her smaller body with his and twined his fingers through hers. He closed his jaw over the muscle between her neck and shoulder and began driving into her, stroke after powerful stroke.

Feeling her clenching around him, he thrust once, twice, three rapid thrusts and then he came, wrapping their arms around each other and holding on tight. His groans were muted by her shoulder.

"Oh, wow," she croaked.

Carefully, he eased out of her and lifted her to his chest. Her head lolled against his shoulder.

"You okay?" He kissed her forehead and laid her down against the pillows.

"Can we do that again? Later?" She yawned and turned to her side.

"I promise," he chuckled. "Don't go to sleep, I have to clean you up."

"I don't have to be awake for that, do I?" she yawned again and curled into a ball.

* * * *

Tracey helped Tav clean up after supper that night and he even let her help put the kids to bed. She found that absurdly funny.

"To think, I've been trying to get out of cleaning up after supper for years and now I'm begging to help! It's too funny!" she chortled.

"This is all part of your devious plan, isn't it?" he laughed at her. "You're like a finicky cat. You want me to order you to sit on the couch and eat Bon Bons."

"Curses! Foiled again!" she chuckled. "I guess I can't get away with banging my head on the counter a second time."

"Only if you're trying to kill *me*!" he growled at her, scooping her into his arms.

"Where are you taking me?" she squealed as he strode toward her bedroom.

She was even more surprised when he averted his course and marched her into the bathroom. "You definitely need a master bathroom," he muttered, sitting her down on the closed seat of the toilet.

He leaned over and turned the shower on and then whipped his shirt over his head. Turning to her, he peeled off her robe and pulled her tee shirt over her head. With a grin, she shimmied out of her panties.

"Your pants are going to get wet, Tavist," she teased, tugging at the waist of his jeans.

"I'm not getting in there. I'm just going to help *you* get all clean," he laughed.

"Oh, no! If *I'm* getting in there, *you're* getting in there!" she declared with a glint in her eye.

"The point of this exercise, fair lady, is to make sure you're squeaky clean," he rumbled.

"You'll do a much better job if you supervise closely," she observed, taking one of his flat nipples into her mouth.

"You're insatiable, woman!" he growled, unbuttoning and unzipping his pants and stepping out of them.

"It's your fault. I'm never like this." He turned and lifted her into his arms once again, stepping under the steamy spray with her. "I love it when you get all he-man on me," she mumbled against him as he let her slide down his body.

"Oops," he whispered, moving both of them around under the warm stream. "I forgot to get a wash cloth."

"No you didn't." She cut a look over at him and grabbed the soap.

Before she let him guess what she had in mind, she soaped him from toes to chest and then began rubbing her body all over him.

With a rumbling growl, Tav lifted her and ordered, "Put your legs around me."

She did and he lowered her down his belly and onto the bulbous tip of his shaft. She felt herself opening for his hard length as she slid down onto him. Soon he was deeply inside her and she wrapped her arms around his shoulders barely able to catch her breath.

He began to move in a slow steady rhythm, the warm water cascading over them. He pressed her against the tile wall, cupping her bottom and thrusting up into her as she clung to him, gasping and mewling with pleasure.

She felt him getting bigger, longer and wider as she clutched at him feeling her release grip her and squeeze. Her entire body seemed to clench and fly apart as she screamed his name. He pumped himself into her rapidly and he too, found his climax.

He held her there for long minutes, not moving. Finally, he carefully lifted her off of him and held her against him as he soaped her body and her hair, then rinsed her off. Without a word, Tav carried her into the bedroom and dressed her for bed.

More than bemused, Tracey was confused. Tav made her feel so wanton and sexy that she didn't even know herself with him. She wanted to put it down to her brain injury but she knew she was in love with Tavist Darke.

Chapter 10

Tracey had fallen asleep almost immediately upon crawling into bed the night before. When Ashley came in to kiss her goodbye, Tav was, of course, busy helping the little girl get ready for school.

Tracey couldn't be certain if he'd spent the night in her bed or not. She wasn't sure why that should bother her but it did. If she was honest with herself, she was looking for a reason to be angry at Tav.

She hadn't asked him to sleep in her bed last night so it would be presumptuous if he had. On the other hand, he'd had sex with her twice. Wasn't she good enough to sleep beside? She was so confused.

When she forced herself to get up and go into the kitchen, she found the house empty. Looking out the window, she saw the boys playing at the edge of the woods. The mail was on the table and she flipped through it. Tav came into the kitchen from the back porch and took her into his arms.

"Good morning, Tracey," he greeted her, kissing her mouth.

She grumbled something but it made no sense to her so she knew he couldn't understand her. He rumbled a laugh at her and left her alone. She began flipping through the mail and stopped short.

Most of her correspondence was bills and junk mail but one letter was personally addressed and had been forwarded from her old home. With shaking hands, she opened it.

Scanning the page, she felt the blood drain from her face. Tav was just coming in the door so Tracey bolted into the bathroom with her letter and the envelope it came in.

Seating herself on the edge of the tub, Tracey turned the shower on and reread the letter. *Hey Babe,* Jack had written, *The waiting is almost over. Daddy's coming home! Boy do I have a surprise for you. Make sure you dress up pretty for me. You'd better be alone. If there's anyone else besides you and my kids, I won't like it. I won't like it at all. I'm afraid I might lose my temper. We don't want that, do we? You know how I am when I build up a real head of steam. It'd be a shame if anyone got caught in the blast, now wouldn't it?*

He'd signed the letter, *Your ever lovin' husband, Jack*

It wasn't hard for Tracey to read between the lines. He was going to find a way out of prison and he would find her. He would find the kids. He expected her to come along quietly or there'd be hell to pay.

If there was a man in the picture, Jack would kill him. One thing she could honestly say about her ex-husband. He was a man of his word. A real mean asshole, yes, he was that, too, but if he said he would do something, you could count on it. It scared her, though. Jack had his own definition of truth, and it didn't always agree with the facts. While she'd learned to decipher his beliefs and implications, she knew it was learned and nobody else would understand. She had to do something, and soon.

Tracey began to tear the letter and the envelope into little pieces. One at a time, she let the shreds of paper wash down the drain of the tub. At first, she stared at them, mesmerized.

When she released the last torn scrap and saw it swirl down the drain, she snapped back to reality. *Tavist!* Jack would kill him. She had to outrun Jack. She had to take the kids and get away. It was her job to keep them safe. It was also her job to keep Tavist safe.

Stepping out of her robe, Tracey took a quick shower. Finished, she pulled the robe back on and hurried back into her bedroom to think. As the day wore on, she acted more cranky and unapproachable. By the time Ashley came home that afternoon, everybody was avoiding her.

She'd come to her decision and she knew it was the right thing to do. She couldn't take a chance on Tav suffering at Jack's hands. She and the kids would have to sneak off alone. Her heart was breaking but she forced herself to be strong.

What doesn't kill you; only makes you stronger. Tracey had learned this over the last few years and believed it wholeheartedly. She knew that her children were counting on her to be strong and protect them. She'd do whatever it took to make sure they were safe, no matter what she had to sacrifice for herself – and of herself.

Throughout the day, Tav had bravely made a few conversational gambits. By the time supper was over and the sky was darkening, even he was taking the long way around her.

* * * *

Ashley and Jacob were sitting side by side on the back porch while Christopher played near the edge of the woods with his toy trucks. Tav had seated himself in the kitchen facing Tracey.

I hope I can do what I need to do here.

He had just opened his mouth to speak when he suddenly jerked his head around.

Shooting to his feet, he ripped his shirt off running out the back door as he went. Following him, she heard it, too. The sound was somewhere between a woman's angry scream and the sound of a saw blade whipping back and forth. She thought she'd faint when she saw the mountain lion crouched to attack Jacob and Christopher.

Tracey barely had time to register alarm as she saw Tav leap into the air a half-naked man and land on the ground as a large, black wolf. He began barking at the huge cat as it pounced and he leaped forward and met it in the air, knocking it sideways, away from the boys.

The large wolf, Tracey couldn't think of it as Tav, rolled over with the mountain lion, jumping away and back again. Continuously barking, snarling, and snapping the lupine herded the lion away from the boys and into the woods.

Jacob had rushed forward to help his brother when the strange animal first appeared. Now he wrapped his arms around the stunned three-year-old and tried to pull him away. Ashley ran forward and added her strength. Before they could get far, Tracey darted from the porch and grabbed at all three of her children, catching a sleeve, an arm, tugging at a length of hair, pushing and pulling them toward the safety of her house.

Suddenly they all froze as a pain filled yelp was heard, followed by another eerie scream. The scream seemed to be moving away from them. Less then a minute later, the large black wolf emerged from the woods.

Ashley and Jacob broke away from Tracey and ran to the animal, babbling and kissing it while it licked them. Christopher struggled to be set on his feet but Tracey wasn't letting go of her baby boy.

"Get in the house, Jacob! Ashley!" she half sobbed, half barked. "Right now!" *If I don't do this now while I'm high on adrenalin, I never will.*

Bewildered, brother and sister reluctantly left Tav and headed for the door. "Take Christopher," she ordered, placing the crying little boy on the porch. Ashley picked him up and took him inside.

Once the kids were in the house, Tracey grabbed Tav's jeans and threw them at him. "Don't come back here," she growled.

He looked at her, confused. As she watched, his form wobbled and he changed from the wolf back into the man she'd made love with, twice.

"Tracey? What?" He pulled his pants on and rose to his feet, taking a step toward her.

"Don't come any closer," she warned, her voice breaking, eyes streaming.

"I told you I was a werewolf. You said you didn't care," he sounded stunned, words slurring slightly.

"I didn't believe you. I thought it was part of my injury." She looked at him, fighting back tears. *Don't lose it now Tracey. You're almost home.* "I didn't know you were a – a freak of nature."

Tav stumbled, his head rocking back as if she'd hit him. He appeared to be struggling to breathe.

Somehow, Tracey held her head up and managed to walk up the stairs to the porch and into the house. She made it into the bathroom and turned the water on before she fell apart.

* * * *

Tav staggered backward into Myles. Myles had heard his friend barking and the mountain lion's scream and had launched himself toward Ashley's house.

When he realized that the children were safe and the mountain lion was gone, he'd turned to head back to Tav's place. But then he heard Tracey tell Tav not to come back. He froze, stunned. The sound of Tav's labored breathing spurred him to turn back toward the little house.

When he heard what his mate's mother said to the most selfless Were he'd ever met, Myles found himself fighting to breathe. He caught Tav as the other man stumbled backward.

At first, Myles thought Tav's weakness stemmed entirely from the words Tracey had flung at him. No doubt those words were the reason why he didn't begin to heal right away, but they weren't the only cause of his stumbling.

Myles realized, looping an arm around Tav that he was bleeding from a gaping wound in his side. The big cat had come close to gutting him.

Deciding that his sports car would be too uncomfortable, Myles carried Tav to his own vehicle, a ramshackle pickup truck. He realized too late that his reclining bucket seats would have been better for Tav than the bench seat of the thirty-year-old truck.

There was nothing else to do but get moving, so he looped a seatbelt around his pack-brother and put the battered old warhorse in gear. Odd jobs had taught him how to drive a manual transmission, thankfully, so he managed to get underway without jostling his passenger too much.

Blood was still oozing from Tav's gaping wound, dark and thick, when Myles squealed to a stop in front of the emergency room doors. It was the same hospital that Tracey had spent a week in, leaving only two weeks prior.

The bustling triage center seemed to screech to a halt when he carried Tav through the sliding double doors. When an orderly ran up to him Myles refused to put Tav down.

"Dr. Montgomery!" he growled. The orderly stood frozen. Myles bent toward him. "Where?" he snarled. "Dr. Montgomery!"

"Right this way, sir." The frightened orderly had probably decided Myles should be the problem of someone who made more money than he did.

Myles didn't care what the young man had in mind as long as he found a Montgomery doctor or someone who could help Tav. He knew he was losing the battle against his emerging beast.

"What's going on here? Oh, dear Lord!" A man slightly older than Myles came rushing in. "Put him right here, sir," he directed Myles.

Myles was glad to cede responsibility for his friend – his brother – to someone who seemed to know what to do for him. He gently laid Tav down on the hard examining table.

The doctor immediately began issuing orders and asking questions of Myles.

"Where's his mate?" the man asked, not looking at Myles.

"She's human," he barked.

"He got family?" the doctor looked at him and looked away.

"I'm his brother," Myles growled.

"He's a Montgomery?" the man asked.

"Adopted Alpha," Myles snarled at him menacingly. "I'm about to call my dad. You want to hear it from him?"

"Mik?" he squeaked. Clearing his throat, he asked again, "Mik Montgomery?"

Myles leaned forward and plucked the cell phone from the doctor's shirt pocket. He quickly jabbed in the telephone number and waited. He began speaking as soon as he heard the voice on the other end.

"Riker, I'm at the Dahlonega hospital with Tav. Mountain Lion. Bring Dad, he needs blood." Myles hung up the phone and dropped it back into the man's pocket.

The doctor began shaking and turned away from Myles. "Take some blood from Mr. Montgomery for his brother. Tape up the wound enough to get him into surgery."

Chapter 11

Ashley helped Jacob and Christopher get ready for bed. She knew her mother would need the help since she'd sent Tav away. She was mad at her mother but she loved her. She wanted her to be okay. She went into the living room to check on her.

Tracey's swollen eyes widened when she saw her daughter. "Ashley!" she shrieked. "You're bleeding!"

"That's not my blood, Mama," Ashley said gently. "It's Tav's blood."

Immediately, Tracey began heaving in great gulping sobs. "I had to do it, I had to…Oh my God, Ashley…"

At first her mother's hysteria scared her. Ashley wasn't sure what to do. Under other circumstances, she'd call Tav or maybe even Myles. That was probably not a good idea right now. She didn't even know if Tav was alive.

That thought scared her as much as her mother's hysteria so she shook her head, forcing her mind away from it. She considered calling Sue but remembered that Sue was away on a big boat for a whole month.

Ashley put her arms around her mother and said, "I'm sure it'll all be okay." *Isn't that what grown-ups always say when they don't really know? I'm not supposed to have to deal with this stuff yet.* "Let's get you to bed. A goodnight's sleep is what you need." *What else? Oh yeah!* "Everything will be much better in the morning, just wait and see." She kept her voice soothing and low the way her mother always did when she was upset.

Tracey followed the little girl to the master bedroom and crawled under the blankets. She was asleep before Ashley left the room.

Ashley had every intention of taking a bath but she decided to sit down on the couch for a minute to think about things. Jacob shook her awake in the small hours of the morning.

"Ashley, we have to go check on Tav. Ash! Wake up!" he shook her again.

"I'm awake, for peep's sake!" Ashley snapped, pushing her long hair out of her eyes and sitting up. "Are you dressed? I wish I knew how to make coffee. Grown-ups really like it when they're tired."

"I got your shoes, Ash. You shouldn't drink coffee. I heard it'd stump your growing. Mama drinks it and look how little *she* is." Jacob had begun putting Ashley's shoes on her feet. He obviously didn't have the patience for her to wake up.

Once the two got outside, after a fair amount of tugging on Jacob's part, they turned toward the path between their house and Tav's. Ashley was almost at the path when she realized that Jacob wasn't with her any longer. Looking back she saw him hesitate a few feet away.

"Ash, what if that great big jaguar, um lion-cat is still there?" Jacob hated revealing weakness but Ashley knew he needed help. It was dark out still, so Ashley couldn't see his blush, but she knew it was there. Jacob had fair skin, he always got real

"Don't worry, Jacob." She walked back to him and took his hand in hers. Once again she reached for the grownup within. "Tav scared it real good. And if it made Tav bleed, I bet Tav made it bleed too." Jacob still seemed nervous. "We can't let one single jaguar keep us from going on our business, can we?"

"No, of course not. Let's go!" He squeezed her hand in a thank you and they took the short walk to Tav's house.

The light was on when they got there and that made Ashley feel better. Maybe Tav wasn't hurt at all.

Brother and sister stood at the porch steps debating whether to call out or knock when the door opened. They whipped around.

"Tav? Myles?" They called.

"You must be Tracey's pups. Jacob and Ashley?" a deep rumbling voice answered.

It made Ashley nervous and she wanted to go, but Jacob wouldn't let go of her hand.

"We're not 'zactly pups," Jacob clarified. "We can't turn into anything…"

* * * *

"Umm, we just wanted to check on Tav. Is he okay?" That trembling little feminine voice had to be Ashley.

"Why don't you two come on in here, hmm? It's really early to be out. I bet you were afraid of finding another mountain lion, weren't you?"

Mik stepped away from the door and the two children trooped in. The smell of Tav's blood was strong on the little girl.

"Ash wasn't but I was. Wow, you're really big. How big are you when you're not a wolf?" Jacob stared at him and Mik thought he was wonderful.

"I'm always a wolf. I don't change," Mik explained.

"That must be really imcon…that must be a real pain, huh?" Ashley asked him.

"Yeah, it has its down sides," he agreed.

"I bet you wish someone would make you some coffee? I will if you tell me how," Ashley bargained.

Mik began to smile. Before he could answer her, the boy, Jacob spoke up.

"Ash, it's gonna stump your growing! You'll be as short as Mama when you grow up!"

"I'm really tired, Jacob. Leave me alone before I get all crabbly like Mama, too!" she snapped.

Mik couldn't help it and he threw back his head and laughed. "I'd love some coffee young lady. Don't worry, Ashley, short women make men feel big and manly. You'll be fine."

Walking with him into the kitchen, she turned to him. "Myles already likes me. He'll like me even if I'm not that tall."

"Fill that thing with water," he said nosing the glass carafe. "What difference does it make if Myles likes you, sweetheart?"

She looked at him and rolled her eyes turning to fill the container with water. "I'm supposed to marry Myles when I grow up. Now what do I do with it?"

"Dump it in there," Mik told her indicating the coffeemaker. He nudged the can of coffee over and picked up a stack of filters with his teeth, dropping them in front of the coffeemaker. "Did Myles tell you that?" he asked.

She took a filter and found the basket to fit it into. "How many scoops? No, I just know."

He looked at her for a minute, unblinking.

"How many scoops?" she asked again.

"Four or five," he answered her. "How do you just know, honey?"

She looked at him for a long time as if considering. Finishing her task, she pushed the button and turned. Jacob came in and sat at the table. Ashley moved to stand behind him and kissed the back of his head in a very adult fashion. She slid into the chair next to his.

"When I was real little, up until I was seven my dad used to hit me. He hit Jacob and he hit Mama, too. He even tried to hit baby Christopher."

Mik sat perfectly still unsure of what this explanation had to do with Myles but he was still glad she was telling him. In another adult gesture, Jacob reached over and squeezed his sister's shoulder.

"Jacob and me, we learned to pay attention to our built in stuff so we wouldn't get hit so much. My teacher says all animals have int stinks."

"Ink stains?" Jacob asked, confused, his brow furrowed in a picture of bewilderment.

"No, dummy, int stinks," Ashley countered. "That's our built in stuff. It tells us when to eat and when to hide."

Mik cleared his throat. "Instincts," he corrected absently. He thought that maybe he was beginning to understand.

Jacob shrugged and continued with the joint explanation. "Ashley and me found out we could smell a bad mood comin'. We could hear anger comin' up the hall," he explained.

"We can't hear and smell the same as Tav or Myles..." Ashley began.

"Or you," Jacob interrupted.

Ashley turned to smile at her brother with a nod, and then turned back to Mik. "You can smell friends and enemies. You can smell love and hate. But a mate is more than a smell -- it's a feeling inside you. Tav is Mama's mate. I know that Myles is mine."

Mik was more than astounded. He was flabbergasted. In a daze he made his way to the coffee pot and, carefully taking the reinforced coffee pot in his teeth, poured himself and the child a mug of coffee. He added milk to both cups and carried them carefully to the table.

How was it that these two little children knew so much, felt so much, and accepted so much? The entire situation was extraordinary. There was almost a feeling of destiny about them...

"We came to find out how Tav is," Jacob's reminded Mik. The little boy's voice jerked him back to the present. "And we really ought to know who you are, shouldn't we Ash?"

"This stuff keeps you awake because it tastes awful, right?" Ashley sputtered, clearly new to the world of coffee drinkers.

Mik grinned, shaking his head. He nudged the sugar toward her, knowing she probably needed it for more than masking the taste of the coffee with all the shocks she'd dealt with in the last several hours. He was sure that, if their mother was anywhere near as endearing as these pups, he knew he'd love her as much as he was beginning to love them. The poor things had had so much to worry about in less than a decade. He hated that Tav had been hurt, but he would bet that there a deeper reasoning behind Tracey's behavior. And of course, he'd always been a sucker for a damsel in distress, just like Tavist.

He knew Myles was outraged on Tav's behalf about what he'd heard Tracey say to him. That warmed him because he knew it was the difference between pack-mates and brothers. A pack-mate would be mad but a brother would be injured.

Mik was beginning to understand why Tracey had said the admittedly abhorrent things she'd said. She'd learned the hard way that even her instincts weren't foolproof.

"Is Tav dead?" Ashley asked point blank. After a long beat of silence she blurted, "And who are you?"

Once again, Mik had been woolgathering. "I'm sorry, child. I'm Mik Montgomery. Myles, Tav, Lakon, and Riker are all my boys. My grandsons call me Gandad. You can call me that too if you want."

The two kids looked at him for long seconds and then nodded. "What about Tav?" they asked together.

"Tav was hurt and he lost some blood but he'll live. He's at the hospital where your mama was."

"We have to go before Mama wakes up," Jacob said in a worried voice.

"Ashley, you should probably change when you get home, honey." Mik looked at her bloodstained clothing.

"Mama saw me last night after Jacob and Christopher went to bed. She thought I was hurt so I told her it was Tav's blood." Her little voice wobbled. "I thought she was gonna stop breathing, she was crying so hard."

Mik watched as the girl stood and drank her coffee without pausing. "Are you okay, Ashley?" He moved over to her and scooped her against him with a large paw.

"I don't know why Mama said those mean things to Tav. She said she *had* to," Ashley mumbled into his fur, beginning to shake. "I just know she won't be okay if he doesn't come back anyway."

The little girl started sobbing into his chest and he looked up and saw Jacob wobbling on the precipice. He held his paw out and the little boy ran to him putting one arm around his neck and the other around his sister. He held both children as they cried.

As he comforted the weeping children, Mik considered their emotionally scarred mother along with the young man he loved like his own son. Jack Aschtholdt, or Jack Asshole as he preferred to think of him, had much to answer for. He hoped he'd get to put his jaws around that man's neck someday.

Eventually he sent Jacob and Ashley home, promising to talk to their mother later while keeping the secret of their early morning visit. First he called the hospital to check on his boys.

He was assured that Riker was putting everyone through their paces and Myles and Tav were both resting comfortably. Myles had given Tav a large amount of blood. Mik had also donated plenty of blood to the cause before he'd come back to Tav's house.

* * * *

Tracey had been sorting through her family's things all morning. She didn't want to move anything that she didn't have to. They'd be on the run again and the less they took with them, the better.

She'd weeded out clothes too small for Christopher and Ashley, putting them aside to give to a shelter. They weren't new enough or nice enough to sell, though there were a *few* things that might be taken by a consignment shop. There was a box on Jacob's bed where she was putting things that were too small for the six year old. Christopher would grow into them.

Jacob had asked her what she was doing and she'd told him she was spring-cleaning. Ashley had roused from her lethargy long enough to caution her mother to take it easy and not to overdo it. Her daughter was the most responsible eight year old Tracey had ever met. She often wondered if it was part of her personality or if the life they'd led had caused Ashley to become that way. She also knew it would only be a matter of hours before the children realized what was going on—that they would be moving again.

Tracey looked in on the kids when the phone rang. She'd kept Ashley home from school and she and her brothers were lying on the floor watching *Sesame Street* reruns. It was an odd day that Ashley didn't want to go to school, especially since she'd been assigned a part in the school play. But even Christopher seemed subdued today. Last night's events had taken a lot out of her children.

Turning, she answered the phone expecting a tele-marketer. She knew Tav wouldn't call. She didn't even know how he was.

"Hello," she said, thinking it would probably be a short call.

"Hello, Tracey. This is Mik Montgomery. I wanted to give you a call and check on you."

"Oh, no! Is Tavist... Is he?" Tracey felt her throat close up. She was shaking like a leaf.

"It's okay, Tracey. Calm down, Honey." The deep baritone voice of Mik Montgomery was soothing and she felt herself relax a little.

"Is he? Mr. Montgomery please, how is he?" she whispered.

"He'll be fine, Honey," he soothed. "He lost some blood but he'll probably be home by tomorrow."

"Thank God," she breathed.

"Tracey, you don't sound like a woman who hates Tav because he's a werewolf," Mik observed.

Although she was relieved that Tav would be okay, nothing else had changed. Thinking fast, Tracey scrambled for the right words to offend this nice man and his wonderful family.

"You're wrong, sir. I *do* hate werewolves. Dog hair makes me sneeze." She thought frantically, "And...and the flea and tick problem around the kids, I just can't have that." *What else, damn, I've never had a dog...* "Digging and chewing and chasing the neighbors' cats. I just can't have that sort of thing. It's better this way. Just..." her voice cracked, "Take care of Tavist for me, please."

She hung up the phone and headed for the bathroom. Tav had been right – she really needed a master bathroom. Maybe their next house would have one, but she couldn't think about that now.

When her tears ended, she washed her face, looked in on the kids again, and booted up her computer. The rest of the afternoon she continued to prepare for moving and looked for places to go.

* * * *

Mik hit the button on the speakerphone and looked at his three boys. Myles face was thunderous. He'd walked in just when Tracey had answered the phone. Tav's eyes swam with tears. He was still pretty weak.

"Dog hair doesn't make her sneeze. Besides, she doesn't even like cats…" Tav trailed off. He turned his head away and gritted his teeth, obviously in emotional pain.

"Maybe so, little brother," Riker chuckled, "But, women hate it when you dig up their flowers and chew up their shoes, just ask Bethany." He squeezed Tav's shoulder.

"Not to mention the ticks and fleas…" Mik rumbled a laugh.

"Ashley wasn't in school today," Myles announced. "The school secretary asked me to tell Tracey that they could only forward Ashley's records to another school." He looked around the room, his mouth tight. "She's going to have to talk to the School Board Superintendent if she wants them when she withdraws Ashley on Friday."

"Oh, God," groaned Tav. "She *does* hate me…She's leaving."

"Think about it, son," growled Mik. "She's leaving without a forwarding address. She thinks she's hurt and offended you so bad that you'll be glad to see her go."

"You're not after her," Riker reasoned, catching on. "She's not running from you."

"Tonight I'll take a look around and see what I can find out around her house," Mik told them. "You get some sleep," he said to Tav. "We need to bring you home by tomorrow morning."

"You should heal faster knowing that she really doesn't hate you, mate," Myles told him.

Tav looked into his eyes. "You really don't think she meant what she said?"

"She's *your* mate. Think about it."

Myles squeezed his shoulder and left the room. Riker joined him in the hall.

Mik put his paws on the bed and leaned down to give Tav a lick on the forehead. "She told Ashley that she *had* to do it, son. She was hysterical when she realized you were hurt. She needs you, Tavist. Those pups need you." He butted foreheads with him and left the room.

In the hallway, Riker and Myles were chatting quietly.

"Myles, you can't hold it against her. Women do ridiculous things to protect their children…"

"You didn't hear her, mate. She called him a freak of nature. That's bullocks, Riker. You'd never stand for it, you know it."

"She's your mate's mother, Myles. You'll have to…"

"I don't think we can track down that ex-husband without Tracey's help," Mik said, interrupting them. "Maybe we should try anyway though," he mused. "Riker what do you think? Myles? I'm sure he's at the root of all this."

"I agree that he's the problem but the kids dunno where he is exactly. Ashley told me he moved from one jail to another and now her mum just tries to make sure *he* can't find *them*," Myles informed them somberly. "Riker's going to toddle on home and round up the troops. We can sort it all out later, I guess," he finished with a shrug.

"I'll just return that rental car at the airport when I go, so I won't need a ride. I'll tell Mom what's going on," Riker spoke finally. "I just want everyone ready in case something happens."

"Don't tell your mother about what's going on here until you have to, son," Mik instructed him in a wry tone. "None of us needs that!"

Breaking up the discussion, Mik and Myles headed to Tav's house and Riker turned his car toward Atlanta. Mik hoped that Tav would sleep long and deeply. The wound was healing nicely and he'd be home in a day or so. It couldn't be soon enough, though. Mik knew in his bones that things were about to get complicated.

Chapter 12

Everything was going smoothly. Jack couldn't have choreographed it better. His waist was fastened to that of six other men. Five of those men had been handpicked for this escape. It was going to be so easy.

Whit Larson, the man next to Jack, was his cellmate. Whit was a follower and a good man to have at your back. He took on Jack's causes and opinions as if they were his own. Vernon Bateman, called Verb for short, was next on the string. Verb was trustworthy, if uppity.

The two men after Verb in the human chain were called the twins. Al Washington was black, wiry, and high strung. The man called his twin, Del Keys, had a mop of dirty blonde hair. He was thick and solid, and very laid-back. They were called the twins because of their evil natures. Either one would be glad to kill a man just to move up in line.

They all knew that Rusty, the sixth man, was a wild card. Nobody was really worried. One sound out of him and they'd knock him out. If they killed him, well—accidents happen. Len Lindsay, last on the string, was quiet and moody. All Jack knew was that he hated being locked up and he had a real grudge against woman of any size or age. That was all Jack really needed to know.

The guards were talking to each other and weren't really focused on the crew. The hash wagon should be along in a few minutes.

The men working this highway maintenance assignment were all considered low risk. Most of them were non-violent, repeat offenders. They had been considered non-violent because their convictions were based on drugs charges or thefts. The title "non-violent offenders" was ridiculously misleading.

Most of the men on the crew were, in fact, very violent. The prison hierarchy had taught them more about violence and abuse than they had already learned in a lifetime. Sure, a man could be rehabilitated if he wanted to be. None of Jack's comrades cared to be rehabilitated. The fact that he'd recently been transferred down from a more secure facility as a result of good behavior simply tickled Jack pink.

When the hash wagon pulled up, the guards, like Pavlov's legendary dogs, responded predictably. They walked around to the order window without a second look toward the men under their supervision. Jack and his six companions turned and began walking into the woods.

"Hey!" squeaked Rusty realizing what was going on, and then his lights went out.

All in all, it was an absurdly easy escape. Most of the guards had been focused on the hash wagon. A convenient shoving match on the other end of the line had distracted the few others. When they were discovered, Jack was certain that the hue and cry would be a quiet one. After all – they were non-violent prisoners, no need to cause a panic, right?

The plastic tie-strips connecting each man to the one next to him allowed them all a great deal of freedom of movement. Regardless, they would all be much happier without the restraints – especially those men on either side of Rusty.

About the time the little group happened upon a dilapidated hunting cabin, Rusty began to come around. He immediately began squawking and protesting that he had been due for release.

Foolishly, the poor man declared that he'd turn the other five men in so that the authorities would know that he was innocent. Nobody had ever accused the hapless Rusty of genius. Jack punched the clamoring man in the mouth knocking him backwards.

One of the twins, Al, had found a hunting knife and a whetstone. He began by cutting himself loose, then Jack, and then, finally, Rusty. Jack reached around and snatched the sheet of tarp draped over a wire stretched across the ceiling of the cabin.

Del took the tarp and wrapped it around Rusty, smiling lazily.

"Don't worry, Rusty, you'll still be released today," Jack murmured, stepping back so that he wouldn't get sprayed.

Al stepped forward and plunged the knife into the tarp just below Rusty's ribcage on the left side. He angled it so that it punctured the man's heart. Del put his hand over Al's to help him withdraw it from the sucking wound.

Wiping the knife on the tarp, Al gave Rusty a gentle shove. The man's mouth worked ineffectually as he gasped out his last breaths. He died with a look of surprised disbelief on his face.

"Now," Jack called, clapping his hands loudly. "Who's ready for a road-trip?"

* * * *

"Mom! There's a police car coming down our road!" called Jacob from the side yard.

"Get in the house, boys!" She ordered.

Tracey couldn't imagine anything she needed less, especially right now with Ashley due home from school any minute. One more day was all she needed and then they would be gone.

Just as the Sheriff stepped out of his car, Tracey saw Tav come out of the woods. She was too rattled to be anything but grateful to see him. Tav walked to her as if nothing had happened and kissed her forehead, turning to the officer.

"Timmons," he growled.

"Darke," snarled the Sheriff angrily in return. "This doesn't have to do with you. Move along."

Tav stepped forward, chest to chest with the Sheriff and rumbled in a low, animalistic growl. Timmons looked Tav in the eyes for long moments. *Am I imagining things? It looks like Tavist is getting bigger.* The Sheriff dropped his eyes first.

"She's my mate. Now talk." Tav's voice was deeper than usual.

"Seven men have escaped from a prison work crew. Jack Aschtholdt was the ring leader." He handed Tav a stack of faxed photos.

Tracey's heart dropped to her toes. The Sheriff's next words turned her to ice.

"Last night, Sue Capitello's home was broken into." Tracey gasped and grabbed Tav's arm.

"Mik! Myles!" Tav called. He didn't yell. He called the two names as if the men were only a few feet away.

Tracey looked and saw a giant silver wolf accompanied by Myles.

"Tracey's ex has escaped from prison. Her friend Sue's house was broken into." Looking at the Sheriff again, Tav asked Tracey, "Wasn't Sue supposed to be away?"

Still keeping his eyes trained on his little notebook, the Sheriff seemed to break out in a sweat. "That's right, she wasn't at home at the time."

Tracey nearly fell over when the large wolf spoke. "Sheriff, I'm Mik Montgomery."

"Yes, sir," the Sheriff's voice had a high-pitched squeak to it.

"This place is about to be overrun with Livingstons and Montgomerys."

"Yes, sir," the Sheriff answered, clearing his throat.

"You be sure and let your pack know they need to identify themselves. Anybody strays too close to Tav's property, his mate, or one of his human pups puts his life in jeopardy, you understand?"

"Yes sir, I understand completely." Wiping his face with a handkerchief, the Sheriff began moving toward his vehicle.

"Where's Ashley?" Myles barked.

"I got a man up on the road," the Sheriff told him, fidgeting with his keys.

"Bloody hell!" growled Myles. "That's just going to scare her."

Before he could take a few steps, Ashley came running into the yard. She stopped, frozen, when she saw the crowd in front of her.

"What's going on?" she asked, her voice a hoarse cry. "What's wrong?"

"Go on!" Mik barked at the officer.

Before Tracey could answer Ashley, Myles stepped forward holding his hand out. "Ashley, I have to tell you something."

When Tracey would have spoken, Tav grabbed her arm and shook his head, holding her back. Tracey was too surprised to respond.

Slowly, Ashley moved to Myles and hesitantly put her hand in his. He got down on one knee and looked into her eyes. The Sheriff drove away.

"Something bad has happened," Myles told her. Her eyes were large and round but she nodded, holding onto Myles's hand, standing just beyond his knee.

"What's wrong, Myles?" She looked at her mother, Tav and Mik, then back at Myles. "Why was the police guy here?"

"Your father escaped from jail, Princess. He could be looking for your family," Myles told her gently.

She began to shake. Carefully, Myles pulled her close to him and stroked her hair and back. After a minute, he tilted her face up. She was gripping the front of his shirt in her fists.

"You know I'm going to take care of you, don't you?" Myles asked her. "You're my little Princess and I'm not going to let anyone hurt you ever again. Do you trust me?"

Ashley looked into his whiskey brown eyes for a minute and then she put her arms around him and buried her face in his chest. "I trust you, Myles, but I'm scared." He held her there for a minute, rubbing her back.

Tracey was flabbergasted. She couldn't move as she watched her timid little girl interact with the muscular young man. *Ashley has just hugged that man on purpose and told him she trusted him. I've stumbled into an alternate universe.*

Pulling back, Myles cupped Ashley's chin and tilted her face up. "It's okay to be scared, Princess. But all my brothers will be coming to help. And I bet Grandma Elke will come, too."

"Who is Grandma Elke?"

"She's Mik's wife—my mum, really. Wait till you meet her, she's mad for shopping and hasn't any granddaughters. It'll be brill," Myles explained as he stood and led Ashley into the house, chatting with her in a low, soothing voice.

"Take a minute, son, and round up Riker, Lakon, and Yancey!" Mik called out. Turning to Tav and a bemused Tracey, he said, "I'm going to round up the Montgomery and Livingston packs around here. We'll get someone to stay with Tracey's friend Sue if need be. I'll be back in a while." He began to turn away and then turned back to Tav. "Myles is right, son. Prepare for impact. Your mother's dying to get her hands on those pups." Then he was gone.

Now that Tracey was alone in the yard with Tav, she didn't know what to do. "The kids…" she began.

"Are fine," he countered.

"I sent you away," she whispered.

"I came back," he said, looking down at her. "You can send me away again later, when you're safe. Until then, you're stuck with me."

"I'm really scared, Tav," Tracey murmured.

Tav put his arms around her and held her close. She could hear his heart beating. She couldn't lie to herself anymore. This is what she wanted. Jack be damned.

She wanted Tav's arms around her for all time. It didn't matter that he was a werewolf. Apparently it wasn't all that uncommon a phenomenon. That Sheriff wasn't a bit surprised when that big wolf started talking.

Admitting her feelings to Tav wasn't going to be easy. She'd been pretty mean when she'd sent him away.

"Tavist," she whispered.

"Yes, ma'am?" his voice sounded like a sexy murmur in her ear.

She still didn't look up at him. "I really didn't mean those horrible things I said to you."

He was silent for long moments. Finally, she did look up. Everything she'd ever wanted to see in a man's eyes was there – along with wariness she *didn't* want there. She needed to be completely honest with him.

"I don't care if you can turn into a- a bat. That doesn't matter to me. I *was* stunned and shocked. Maybe, if I didn't already love you, I would have objections to your being a werewolf." When he would have spoken, she placed two fingers on his lips. "I was afraid for you." She paused, thinking about what else she needed to say. Taking a deep breath, she added, "I'm really sorry, Tavist. You're the most human, *humane* man I've ever met. I *do* love you. So much…"

She removed her fingers. With a low, rumbling growl, he pulled her to him. His mouth covered hers in an aching, demanding, passion-filled kiss. When he finally raised his head, she clung to him knowing she'd land in a heap if he made her let go.

"I love you, Tracey West. I will never force you into anything but I won't ever let you go either. You're stuck with me."

* * * *

Holding his trembling mate in his arms, Tav was weak with relief. Gently, he urged her to the porch where they both sat down. Needing the closeness, he lifted her onto his lap.

"You're getting closer and closer to that spanking I promised you a few days ago," he murmured.

"You say it but you don't mean it," she sighed, resting against his chest. "Oh!" she yelped, jumping up.

Before he could say anything, she pulled him to his feet and began tugging at his tee shirt. When she had it un-tucked from his jeans, she pushed it up, examining his abdomen closely.

She found what she was looking for in the thick pink scar that started just below his ribcage and ended parallel to his navel. Pushing him backward to sit on the porch, she stroked and kissed the torn flesh.

"It looks like its healing. I'm so sorry, Tavist, so sorry. Can you ever, ever forgive me? I don't know if *I* can forgive me."

Tav pulled her back onto his lap. "Hush, love," he admonished her. "We need to talk. This little scratch is healing. I'll be fine."

Tracey sighed. "I know, Tavist. I know we need to talk." She closed her eyes and rested her head against his shoulder.

He let her rest for a minute and then he tipped her chin back so he could look into her blue, blue eyes. "Tracey, do you want to live your life with me? Be honest. It's important."

"Of course it's important!" she groused. "What kind of a thing is that to say? Like I don't know what's important and what's not... I *do* have three kids you know!"

Tav shook his head. "Okay, poor choice of phrasing. You didn't answer me. Don't worry, I..."

She reached up and put her hand on his lips again. "Yes, Tavist, I want to live my life with you. I want to have your babies – except we'll need a much bigger house. I want to go to bed with you and wake up with you every single day."

Tav couldn't fight his happy smile and he didn't try. Even though he had a definite agenda for this conversation, he deviated from it long enough to kiss Tracey until she clung to him again.

"We've already mated in the ways of my kind." He knew he looked a little guilty, but only a little. "I put my mark on you the first time we made love." She looked at him with wide round eyes. He moved the neck of her shirt aside and licked her shoulder. "I want to marry you according to your beliefs."

He saw Tracey's eyes fill with tears. He leaned down and kissed each cheekbone. His lips feathered down her jaw and over to her mouth. He nipped at her lower lip and then soothed it with his tongue.

Once again, he sunk his tongue into her velvet mouth and mated his with hers until he could barely breathe. He could feel her shaking with need in his arms. He was heavy and aching but he wouldn't do anything about it yet.

"Tracey," he forced himself to speak. "I can't marry you without a certain promise."

"What promise?" she sounded breathless still.

"You have to promise to come to me right away if anything frightens you or makes you nervous." He took a deep breath. "I don't care if it's high prices at the grocery store or if you think I'm acting badly. Promise what happened three days ago will never happen again."

"Oh, Tavist" she groaned. "I'm so…"

"Tracey!" he growled, cutting her off. "This isn't about fault and blame. It's about both of us feeling safe together. Okay?"

She nodded, tears dripping down her cheeks now. "I promise to always tell you, I promise," she whispered.

Standing, he placed her on her feet. "You've never been to my house, have you?"

She shook her head. He raised his voice just a little. "Myles, we're walking over to my house. I hear Mik coming now."

Taking her hand, Tav led her around the house and down the path. Sure enough, Mik was just coming into the backyard.

"We'll be back in a little while," Tav grinned. He saw Tracey's face flush before she ducked her head in embarrassment.

"Tracey," Mik rumbled, "Welcome to the family."

"Mr. Montgomery, I'm sorry about what I said. I don't…"

"Don't worry, sweetheart, I spoke to Tav about digging, chewing, cat chasing, and good personal hygiene. He's ready to be house trained now."

Mik reached up and licked a red-faced Tracey on the cheek and padded off. Tav grinned and then led Tracey towards his house, but first he showed her a quick tour of his studio. While she asked about his paintings, it dawned on him that soon, one day, he'd like to present her with a family portrait of her own – with her children, herself and him. And he'd paint it with every emotion he had to put in it.

* * * *

Mik was just coming in the back door as Myles hung up the phone. "That was Yancey. He's coming in with Lakon. They'll all be here in a few hours."

"Myles?" Jacob stopped a few feet away from him.

"Yes, Jacob?" he responded. He knew the boy didn't trust him. He wondered if he ever would.

"What's your favorite color?" he looked over his shoulder and back at Myles.

"Green," Myles answered. Seeing the frown on the little boy's face he said, "Dark green, really."

Jacob stomped a foot and flounced back through the doorway. "You were right Ash," Myles heard him say grudgingly. "You were double right. I owe you something else. I already ate my chocolate pumpkin that Uncle Lakon got us."

"I don't need a reward for being right. It's a reward all by itself," Ashley grinned.

From anyone else, Myles was sure that statement would have sounded smug. Coming from Ashley, it sounded like good-natured teasing.

"In Spanish that's *verde*. Dark green is *verde oscuro*. Come on Christopher, find the *verde oscuro* crayon."

Christopher promptly produced a forest green crayon and Jacob and Ashley cheered, hugging and praising him.

Buoyed by their enthusiasm, Christopher picked up the green crayon and toddled over to Mik and Myles announcing, "*Verde* means green!"

"Smashing little man, absolutely smashing! Very bright indeed!" Myles praised him.

He couldn't deny how smart Ashley and her brothers were. He also couldn't deny how good he felt inside when she beamed at him. Giving him a hug, he set the little boy down again.

Christopher grabbed a blue crayon and handed it to Jacob saying, "Blue means *azul!*"

"Blue's my favorite," Jacob allowed.

"Me, too!" clapped Christopher.

Ashley sat down with Christopher again and Jacob moved over near Mik and Myles.

"Do we still have to leave tomorrow?" Jacob asked.

"I say, old chap, why would you want to leave?" Myles patted the couch next to him.

Jacob eased onto the cushion beside Myles and looked at him for a long time. "You don't want us to leave, do you?"

"Right in one, Jacob. I want you to stay right here with Tav. Is that what you want?" Jacob nodded solemnly.

The little boy looked over at Ashley and Christopher. In a low voice, he said, "I heard what that policeman said. Daddy's looking for us, isn't he?"

"He is," Mik nodded, answering him.

Jacob tore his eyes off of his sister and looked into Myles's eyes. "Daddy says girls are only good for one thing and he can cook and clean for himself." He looked back at Ashley. "You have to make sure Daddy doesn't get near her. He hates Ashley."

Myles closed his eyes and counted, holding his breath. When he felt he could speak without sprouting hair on his face he answered Jacob.

"I promise you that I'll keep her safe, Jacob. Do you believe me?"

Jacob smiled a small smile and reached up, touching an elongated canine tooth with his index finger. "I believe you, Myles."

Chapter 13

"I'm glad we could spend a few minutes by ourselves, Tracey," Tav took her hand and led her into his bedroom.

"There are no blankets on the bed," Tracey looked around.

"I get pretty warm," Tav smiled. "Don't worry, I'll keep you nice and toasty." He took her into his arms and pulled her close.

"You will?" she smiled coyly.

"Maybe I'll even make you as hot as you make me," he growled.

"Promises, promises," Tracey giggled. She wasn't used to flirting and she wouldn't try to be someone she wasn't.

Tav put his arms around Tracey and leaned back to look into her eyes. "Tracey? You know for sure that I'm a werewolf. We're considered half man and half wolf. Most people think we're monsters if they think of us at all."

"Tavist, you may be half wolf but you're all man. I love you. I know what you are. Now you know the truth about me." She waited. She knew he'd ask.

"The truth about you?" He didn't let her down.

"I'm half woman, half chicken. Does that make me a werechicken?"

Tav scooped her up growling into her throat and dropped her onto the bed, following her down. "Good thing for you, woman, that I'm a carnivore!"

Tracey had about half a second to speculate on how incredible it was to have such a big, strong, handsome man want her this way, before Tav began undressing her with his teeth.

She lay back and enjoyed that for a few minutes until he got her bra off. She decided she really needed to feel skin against skin. It was nearly impossible to get his shirt off when he wouldn't remove his mouth from her breast – not that she didn't want his mouth there.

Tav stopped nibbling and sucking at her sensitive nipples long enough to pull his shirt over his head. He took that opportunity to pull her jeans and panties and his own jeans off. She wanted to touch him so much.

Tav apparently had other ideas. He took both wrists in one strong hand and held them above her head. He began licking, kissing, and nibbling his way down her body. He was almost at her navel when he had to release her.

By that time, Tracey was senseless. He'd licked the underside of both breasts and nibbled and kissed his way over each and every rib. He'd stopped and paid special attention to the scars she had there.

He kissed over her slightly rounded abdomen and down over one hip, one thigh, her right kneecap – all the way down to her ankle and around it. She was squirming and moaning by the time he made his way up her left leg.

Finally, he began stroking her labia gently with his tongue. The sensation caused her to moan loudly and squirm still more. Tav grabbed her thighs in his strong hands and held them open.

He placed his mouth over her weeping slit and alternated between sucking and plunging his tongue in and out. "*Mmm*," he groaned. "More!"

He began nipping and sucking her little nub and then moved his mouth back to her opening. Rubbing and pinching lightly with one hand, he continued to suck and plunge with his tongue. She came violently and couldn't seem to stop, sobbing out her climax.

Tracey was sure she couldn't possibly feel any further sexual stimulation and then she felt Tav slide up her body.

"Kiss me, Tracey," he rumbled. "Taste how beautiful you are." He covered her mouth with his and swept his tongue between her lips.

She felt the hot liquid gush between her legs at his words. Almost immediately, the rounded head of his hard shaft pushed against her center. She spread her legs and lifted her hips and he slid inside of her to the hilt.

"Good," he groaned. "So good. So beautiful."

He began moving slowly at first and then faster. Soon he was pumping into her with a powerful driving force. She wrapped her legs around his hips and hung on, feeling the heat of tension building inside of her.

Suddenly it felt like a volcano exploding inside of her as her orgasm ripped through her in wave after powerful wave. Tav was still pounding inside of her fiercely, lunging toward his own climax. After a series of mighty thrusts, he came with a roar. He contracted around her and clamped his jaw onto her shoulder, pouring his seed into her.

It took him a few minutes, but with great effort, it seemed, he managed to lever himself off of her pulling her next to him. She could hear the sticky, sweaty sound their bodies made when they moved apart. His breath was still coming in gasps as was hers.

Finally, Tracey forced herself out of bed and Tav followed after her. She insisted that they take separate showers, knowing that they'd never leave if they ended up naked in close proximity again.

* * * *

At Tav's nod, Mik and Myles eased away from the little family. The kids had wanted to play on the swing and the two werewolves had seen no reason why they shouldn't. They were all outside at the tree when Tracey and Tav joined them.

Tracey snuck up behind Ashley and picked her up, swinging her in a circle while Tav reached out and stopped the swing. Jacob held tight to his little brother who squawked in protest.

"Hang on now, buddy!" Tav laughed, reaching over to pluck the two-year-old off of his brother's lap.

Tav lowered himself to sit on the ground holding Christopher. Tracey sunk down with her arms wrapped around her little girl and pulled her onto her lap. Jacob slid out of the swing and sat against the tree-trunk, looking first at his mother and then Tav.

Glancing quickly at his sister, he blurted, "You want to talk about the Sheriff and our dad, right?"

Tracey opened her mouth to speak but Ashley interrupted. "Jacob and me, I mean, Jacob and *I* – um, *we* think you and Tav should get married and we should all just stay here and fight Daddy till he dies or goes away. And then we should live happily ever after…mostly."

Tracey's mouth snapped shut and her eyes caught Tav's. He fought the urge to grin and looked solemnly at the little girl. Transferring his gaze to Jacob, he struggled with laughter as the little boy glared defiantly at him, daring him to argue their logic.

Tav shrugged. Tracey shrugged. "Okay," they said at the same time.

Ashley and Jacob looked at each other for long seconds and then Jacob launched himself at Tav. He fell backwards in a heap with a giggling Christopher squirming against him, laughing uproariously.

Tav fended off the enthusiastic affections of the two boys as he watched Ashley turn in her mother's embrace, and snake her arms around Tracey's neck.

"So this is real? Really real?" Ashley demanded, staring into Tracey's eyes.

"Completely real. No more hiding, no more being afraid. Well, maybe a little but we're not going to be alone anymore." Tracey's gaze didn't move from Ashley's until the little girl collapsed in a relieved sigh.

* * * *

When Elke, Bethany, and Riker arrived, chaos ensued. Yancey and Lakon arrived shortly after them.

Elke swooped in like a hungry eagle, grabbing Christopher and Jacob in a bear hug. She peppered them with kisses as she introduced herself.

"I'm Grandma Elke and I can't wait to spoil you to *death*!" Elke announced. "Where's that precious little girl?"

Tav saw Ashley peek out from behind Myles's legs. That's all the encouragement Elke needed.

"Look at you, you beautiful little thing!" Elke squealed. "Lakon, Riker, just look at her! *Look at her!* Why can't either of you give me a sweet little girl grandbaby, too?"

Ashley was clinging to Myles's legs. Tav could tell that both Ashley and Myles were having a hard time with the influx of people. When Yancey came in the door, Tav knew trouble was brewing.

Myles growled low in his throat when Riker squatted in front of Ashley and said hello. A moment later Yancey stepped up, causing Myles to snarl menacingly. Tav could see his beast emerging and grabbed him from one side and Riker grabbed him from the other. They swept him out the door with Lakon, Mik, and Yancey following.

"What'd I do?" Yancey yelped. "I swear, I really don't know…"

"Don't worry, cuz," Tav told him. "It's okay."

He listened with half an ear while Lakon explained to Yancey what had Myles so upset. Riker headed over to the tree talking to Myles who still wrestled with the beast in him.

"You okay man?" Tav asked him as Myles forced himself to calm down.

"You're going to have to leave here, son. You can't go on like this for very long," Mik told Myles.

Myles laughed humorlessly. "I can just see me ripping the throat out of some ten year old boy for pulling her hair or vivisecting a thirteen year old for trying to steal a kiss."

"Don't think about it, My, it's gonna make you crazy." Lakon was trying to soothe him, with limited success. Tav saw aching sympathy for Myles in the other man's eyes. "We'll be on tour again in a couple of months."

"I know you don't want to leave but…" Riker began.

"Myles?" Tav swore that Ashley was part wolf or part cat. She was always appearing out of nowhere. "Are you going to leave me?"

Looking at the group of werewolves, Tav thought they were frozen in place. Myles was the first to mobilize.

"No, Princess, I'm staying right here until I know you're safe." He'd reached her in a few strides.

Mik nudged Lakon who, with Yancey, followed him into the woods toward Tav's house. Having all of them so close to Ashley right now was just asking for a fight.

Tav and Riker moved around the side. They'd still hear the conversation and Myles knew it. Possibly even Ashley did, Tav wasn't sure. Between Ashley and Jacob, maybe all three children, Tav was convinced they had some sort of seer abilities. There was just something supernatural about them. Half hidden behind a large tree on the edge of the woods, Tav watched Myles take Ashley's hand and sit on the step, pulling her to stand in front of him.

"After that, though, after you think we're safe, you're leaving, aren't you?" Ashley's voice sounded infinitely sad.

"I have to, Princess," Myles sounded desperately sad as well.

"Why, Myles?" she asked simply.

"I have to give you a chance to grow up. If I'm here all the time, you won't get to play and run around like you should," Myles explained.

"I'll run around if you want me to, Myles. You can chase me. We'll have fun." Tav could hear the tears in Ashley's voice.

He heard the swishing sound of fabric against fabric. Myles was hugging the little girl.

"Don't cry, Princess. Someday we'll be together as much as we want. Until then, I'll come to see you on your birthday and when important things happen," Myles promised.

"You mean like the school play and dance recitals?" Ashley asked shyly. "And maybe Christmas and Thanksgiving?"

"That's exactly right. We can write letters to each other, as well. It'll be bee's knees, won't it?" He was obviously trying to sound cheerful.

There was silence for a minute then, "Myles, are you sure bees *have* knees?" she asked skeptically.

"Well I'm not, really, but it would be almost as smashing as having a letter from you in my mail, wouldn't it?"

Tav heard the swishing sound of a hug again. "I'd rather have you here." Her muffled voice sounded very pouty, he thought. He'd never heard Ashley pout. "But, I won't be a big baby, I promise," she said on a very shaky sigh.

"You can be as big a baby as there ever was and you'll still be my little Princess," Myles told her. Tav could hear them standing. "Let's go in and have Grandma Elke spoil you, shall we? You'll be the only girl."

"Spoiling is bad, Myles. If something gets spoiled, Mama usually throws it away." They heard Myles laugh and try to explain how painless being spoiled really was.

* * * *

"Best I can tell, it's a big family-type get together, Jack!" Verb called back in a muted voice. "But I recognize some of em!"

"What do you mean? How do you recognize them? You've never met my wife. Let me see," Jack snapped, tugging Verb back and snatching the binoculars from his friend.

These were one of the treasures they'd taken from Sue's house the day before. Jack figured Sue owed him. For one thing, she'd had a lot to do with his ex-wife's belated bid for freedom.

He also figured she owed him, too, because she hadn't been home. He'd promised the other men some "sport". Since she hadn't been available to participate, his fellow escapees were harder to control.

Carefully, the two men crept closer to the edge of the trees. They felt sure that they still couldn't be seen. Jack fondled the gun in his pocket, the heavy weight giving him confidence and reassurance.

"Welcome to the family, Tracey!" Jack heard one of them men call out. He did a double take, disbelieving what his eyes were telling him. *Goddamn! That's Riker Montgomery!*

As he watched, the actor released two squirming boys who instantly ran at the two boys standing hand in hand behind their mother, his ex-wife. Seeing Riker Montgomery take his wife into his arms for a hug nearly cancelled out his feeling of pride when looking at his sons.

"They look like you," whispered Verb, smiling.

Jack felt a blush creep up his face and couldn't stifle a grin. "Yeah, they do, don't they?" He turned back to look at them again.

"Uncle Riker?" That was Jacob, his first-born, unless you counted the girl—which he didn't.

Jack looked for her, half listening to his son. He spotted the girl standing with a large dog of some kind and two other men. "When Mom marries Tav, that makes Kade and Kam our cousins, right?"

He didn't hear the large man's answer through the pounding in his ears. *Marries who? Doesn't matter, that bitch isn't marrying anybody. She's* my *wife. She's mine and she'll die mine! Soon, probably. Her and that damned girl.*

Jack nudged Verb and carefully walked backward. Verb followed and both men made their way down the hill where they'd been overlooking the gathering. They made their way through the underbrush and back to the other two men as quietly as they could, both considering what was to come.

* * * *

"Wanna follow 'em?" whispered Yancey to Lakon. Both men were in wolf form.

"Naw," we can track 'em later. Let's see if they come back," Lakon answered his cousin quietly.

From the direction of the yard, both Weres heard footfalls heading in their direction. They slowly moved toward the sound.

"Hey, beautiful," Lakon addressed Bethany when she appeared from around a bush.

"Hey Lakon, Yancey," she smiled at both wolves and bent down to scratch behind Lakon's ear. "So what do you think of our new sister?" she asked Lakon.

"Mmm, she's...pretty," Lakon began.

"She's formidable," Bethany laughed. "Your mother has met her match."

Lakon chuckled and then became serious again. "You know, given her history and Jack Asshole's overall – Asshole-ness – she's a lot different than I expected."

"What'd you expect?" Bethany asked curiously. Yancey nodded his curiosity.

"I guess I expected her to be a lot more passive. You know...a lot more downtrodden," Lakon offered.

"Good God, don't let Tracey hear you say that!" Tav said, joining the small group. "She'll have your pelt for a bathmat!"

Yancey and Bethany began to laugh. "Shit, I bet she would," he chuckled. "I heard her say that bathroom needed a little something."

"So what's on tap for tomorrow?" Yancey ventured, scratching his side and yawning loudly.

"Tracey and I are going into town to get a marriage license," Tav grinned. "Myles is going to take Ashley to school and hang out there until she's done. Elke, Bet, and Mik are going to stay with the boys."

"How about I tag along with Myles?" Yancey suggested, "Riker and Lakon," he nodded at his furry cousin, "you guys take the night shift? You can bed down in Tav's studio in the morning."

Chapter 14

It had been a long night and a pretty uncomfortable morning. Their sleeping accommodations had left a little something to be desired, to say the least. Not only that, his "team" was becoming a little impatient with him. Jack was *not* in a very good mood.

"Follow the girl, Ashley, and those two apes!" ordered Jack, not looking back at Al and Del. He'd decided whom each man would follow according to his own personal need for revenge. "I don't care what you do to her, just get rid of her!"

Jack wanted to punish Tracey himself and he didn't care what happened to Ashley, as long as he never had to see her again. As far as he was concerned, all his troubles began with her. If Tracey hadn't gotten pregnant with her, things would have been much better. If Ashley had only been a boy, his parents would have been happier with him, he just knew it. That would have meant money from his parents right off the bat. Chances were he'd never have had to hit Tracey, because she wouldn't have messed up so badly if she'd had the boy first. It was all her fault.

Now, he wanted his sons back and he knew he could count on Len and Verb to get them without hurting them too much. As long as nothing was broken, Jack didn't care. He wouldn't be paying to fix anything, he'd leave the kid behind first. He didn't mind if they got knocked around a bit. It would toughen them up a little—teach them how to be men.

He, Jack, would take Whit and follow the happy couple until they could trap them somewhere. He'd teach that bitch some manners right after he took care of that cocky lothario who thought he was going to marry *Jack's* wife.

"You ready for school, Ashley?" the men heard from the woods overlooking the yard. "Your chariot awaits, Milady!" A youngish man, swept a low bow and held the door open for the little girl.

"The guy looks like that famous sax player…Mike?" Al speculated, nudging Del.

"Myles, I'm pretty sure."

Giggling, Ashley climbed in. Another man scooted in under her, pulling her onto his lap and mumbling about sports cars and tight fits.

He snapped the seatbelt around the two of them as they drove away laughing.

Unknown to them, their sneering audience of two was hiking toward the elementary school. Al and Del had been told that, once there, she'd be there a while.

"Those two louts will probably hang around so just count on that," Jack had warned them. By now, Tracey must know that he was out of prison. He wished he'd had more time to study their daily activities.

To the three remaining men, he said, "Verb, Len, go on back there behind the house. When everything is quiet, just get the boys and meet us up on the road up past the hospital. And watch out for that big dog!"

"Yes, sir!" Verb responded sharply, earning himself an exaggerated roll of the eyes from Len.

"You're such a suck-up, Verb, sheeit!" he groused as the two men disappeared into the trees behind the house.

Ignoring the two squabbling men, Jack kept his eyes trained on the couple strolling slowly up the tree-covered road toward the other house. They were met by another couple – that actor, Montgomery, Riker, Jack noted, and the blonde woman must be his wife, Bethany.

"Mmm…" Grinning and groaning happily, Bethany strolled up to Tav and Tracey and stretched her arms up in the air and settled them around them. "What a beautiful morning!"

"Group hug!" Laughing, Riker came up behind them and wrapped his arms around all three.

"Disgusting!" Jack growled to himself, watching the two couples exchange their morning greetings.

"I'm going to go sit with Elke and the boys," Bethany began. "Riker's going to go over to the studio and join Lakon. They're going to nap." She stood on her toes and kissed her husband's cheek.

Turning to them, Riker explained, "This way you'll have some privacy in case you want to…visit…when you get back from town." He flexed his eyebrows up and down suggestively.

Jack looked on as two people, Tracey and Tav, slid into a battered pick-up truck while the other two walked off in separate directions.

"What we gonna do now, boss?" Whit asked, looking for direction.

"Simple, we're going to go into that house and wait for our prey to return," Jack's grin was feral. "They're going to walk right up to us and hand themselves over. Let's go see what's to eat in there."

* * * *

"Gandad?" Mik heard a quiet whisper. He opened one eye when he felt small fingers in his ear. "*Gandad*!" a little voice whisper-shouted.

He started to speak but a pair of plump little hands stretched around his snout holding it closed. "Shhh, Gandad. The ugly man wants to play. Shh."

Mik narrowed his eyes and looked up at the redheaded cherub seated on his back and draped over his neck. He got an upside down view of Christopher's serious face and managed to mumble, "Where? Which man?" he asked, keeping his voice low and barely moving his mouth.

Christopher slid down Mik's back and looped both arms around him. "There," he whispered, pointing a chubby finger. Mik licked the finger causing the little boy to giggle loudly.

"You go play with him, puppy, I'll go lay down over by the house, okay?" Mik whispered back. He felt uneasy about encouraging the boy to play with an adult stranger but, just this once, it would be necessary. How else could he draw him out? He'd never let Christopher be in any real danger. There were two of them, Mik knew, two strangers nearby, but he couldn't pinpoint the other—they were too close together.

Christopher clapped and nodded, releasing Mik who stood and stretched. Shaking himself out to the accompaniment of the child's giggles, he walked around the side of the house and sat down.

Now he could clearly smell both men and barked a warning yip to Elke. He heard a pan rattle and a low yip of acknowledgement.

He kept the sounds of the boy and the man walking into the woods to his left. For a few minutes, he just moved along with them silently, gliding through the trees as they tromped.

"No!" he heard Christopher's irate voice exclaim. "Put me *down*!" the little boy demanded loudly and angrily. "Gandad!"

"Shut up, ya little bastard! Shut up!" The sound of an open palm striking flesh was heard accompanied by a small boy's wail.

Mik's plan was to separate the two men and Christopher had been cooperating beautifully. There was no reason to hit him – the man couldn't suspect that a werewolf was nearby. Anger shot through the big wolf.

His hackles went up and he bared his teeth. Dropping his head and shoulders low, he began to close in on the fool who'd raised his hand to an innocent child.

Christopher was sobbing and struggling in the man's arms when he caught sight of Mik.

"Gandad!" he cried and bit down on the man's arm with all his might.

"Why you little..." he dropped Christopher, swearing.

"Gandad, Gandad, Gandad!" Christopher repeated, crawling behind the wolf and grabbing his tail.

Ears back, lip curled and brow furrowed, Mik sucked in a large breath and began to snarl menacingly, still advancing.

"Mother of God, Jesus and all the Saints," croaked Verb, his eyes wide as he stumbled backward, obviously in awe of the enormous and angry animal.

"Get 'im, Gandad!" Christopher growled. He placed both tiny hands on Mik's haunch and shoved.

Mik grinned evilly and leaped.

"Bad dog," Verb squeaked right before he passed out.

* * * *

Elke had heard and acknowledged Mik's warning. The idea that *anyone* thought that they could bother her grandchildren just made her mad.

"Bethany, honey, we apparently have uninvited company," she warned her daughter –in-law.

"Jack's kid don't have no yella eyes," Elke heard as she followed Bethany into the living room. "C'mere kid, you got dark hair and dark eyes. You're Jack's."

"Am not!" bellowed Jacob. "Tav's my daddy now! You let me go!"

Two snarling little bodies whirled around the man's legs until a yelp was heard and Kaden went flying backward. Jacob's shouts and Kameron's snarls increased.

"How dare you touch my grandbabies!" roared Elke. She began to change into half-were form and was just glad she was wearing a dress with a long full skirt. *No need to traumatize the little angels by seeing Gramma naked.*

124

She curled her lips and snarled, still changing into half-were form. "You put that boy down, right now!" she barked.

Without a word, Len loosened his arms and let Jacob slide to the floor. Free of the weight of the little boy, he continued backing and stumbling away, wide-eyed and shaking. He lost control of his bladder when his back hit the wall and he could go no further.

"He wet his pants!" snickered Kameron and Kaden who were clinging to Bethany. Kaden had his arm around a stunned Jacob.

As they watched, Elke lifted the terrified would-be kidnapper and tossed him into the yard following him out.

"*That* is so *incredibly* cool!" she heard Jacob exclaim to his new cousins. "Gramma *rules*!"

She was still grinning as she tied the would-be kidnapper's hands behind his back with her apron.

* * * *

"Are you sure you're ready to take on a grouchy redhead and her three troublesome children?" Tracey asked Tav as he started to help her down from the seat of his old truck.

"Piece of cake," he boasted, placing his hands on her waist.

"Anyone ever tell you "you can't have your cake and eat it too?" someone jeered from behind him.

Quickly, Tav pushed Tracey away and began to turn. His blood ran cold as he spotted the gun in the smirking man's hand.

"Uh, uh, *ah*," Jack sing-songed. "That's far enough, Loverboy!" he barked.

Tav took a single step toward him. That's as far as he got before he heard the loud pop of the gun and felt the burning in his shoulder. As the white-hot pain seared him, he sunk to his knees. *Stay there, Tracey, please*. He hoped she would heed his mental warning.

As evidenced by her red, red hair, her temper reigned. Tav groaned when he heard her hop from the seat of the truck and stomp past him.

"How dare you shoot the man I love you – you…You big, fat JERK!" she bellowed.

"Tracey!" he croaked, trying to shake off the pain in his shoulder. "Tracey don't…"

Speech failed him as he watched his fiery mate ignore the gun in the other man's hand and turned marching right up and into his face.

Jack was apparently as taken aback as Tav, seeming to forget the weapon as his mouth dropped open.

Everything moved in slow motion after that, Tracey's arm flexed and pulled back and then she let loose, slugging the other man hard on the side of the mouth with all her might. The strength of the blow lifted him and flung him backward leaving him a groaning heap a few feet away. The gun bounced away and Tav noticed absently that it landed under the truck.

Her temper still simmering, Tracey stomped over to the fallen man and kicked him. "Get up, you bully! I'm not done punching you yet!" She kicked him again, "GET!" Kick, "UP!"

Tav began to chuckle, memorizing the image of his diminutive mate standing over what had been her worst nightmare, kicking him and ordering him to "Get up so I can hit you again!"

He felt the tingle in his shoulder that told him the healing had begun. Pulling himself to his feet, he was surprised by the sound of a strangled gasp coming from the other side of Tracey.

"Boss!" Whit croaked. "*Boss*!" he bellowed.

Before Tav's agile mind could grasp what was happening, Whit backhanded Tracey across the mouth sending her flying backward into a tree. She landed hard and he could see blood pouring from her nose. Her cheek was a deep pink and he knew she'd have a bruise before too long.

Rushing to her side, he checked her pulse and mopped at the blood. She was dazed but okay. Tav felt anger sweep over him.

He began to growl low in his throat as he turned toward the man who'd hit his mate. He felt his fangs lengthen and his nails grow and curve as he advanced, still snarling.

Whit dropped to the ground scanning frantically and spotted the gun under the truck. He scrambled toward it. With a roar, Tav leaped at the retreating man, changing in midair. His powerful jaws closed over the other man's shoulder and clavicle, crushing them and tearing the flesh.

Tav ignored his opponent's screaming as they hit the dirt and he rolled with his enemy until he could get his four legs on solid ground. With a mighty shake, he lifted the wounded man and flung him away.

It had taken great inner strength not to close his jaws over the man's neck. He'd wanted to kill him. Over and over scenes of the bodies of his first mate and his little boy bloodied and unmoving flashed through his mind. Those images were followed by Tracey's face, pale and lifeless, blood dripping down. He fought the urge to dive onto the still form of her attacker and rip through his flesh until he crushed the man's heart between his teeth.

"You okay, son?" Tav turned his bloody face toward the voice of his adopted father. "Son?"

Mik approached him and licked some of the blood from his snout. Tav rested his forehead against the older wolf's brow.

"I'm okay, Mik," he sighed. He felt a large paw come over his back as a tear trickled from his eye. "I'm alright – I – I … I'm fine."

"You're a good man. Go look after your mate. The boys and I'll clean this up for you." With another lick, Mik turned toward Riker and Lakon who were approaching from the direction of the studio.

One of Tracey's kicks had rendered Jack unconscious so when he regained his senses, he was already tied up. Lakon, a recent convert to the versatility of Duct Tape™, had secured the men's wrists, feet, and mouths with the sticky, silver tape. Nobody paid attention to Whit's whimpering and moaning, although Lakon did tape his arm across his chest as if it were in a sling.

* * * *

Myles fought for control as the beefy Sheriff argued with him. The meddlesome Were was blocking his view of Ashley's classroom and his last nerve was rapidly fraying.

"Sheriff Timmons, you were advised that this place would be overrun by Montgomerys. If you don't step aside, I promise you that a melee will ensue," Myles tone was clipped. While he was speaking politely, he could feel his fangs lengthening and feel the hair sprout across his cheekbones.

"This is a public elementary school, Mr. Montgomery. I can't just let you do whatever you want. It's my job to protect these children here," Sheriff Timmons countered in a growl.

"That's bloody well fine, Sheriff. Protect as many as you want. I'm lookin' after just one, so belt up, clear off and let me get on with it!" Myles snarled back, resisting the urge to shove the large man. If he did, he knew the Sheriff would go flying.

"Sheriff, we just need to be able to keep an eye on Ashley West and they're heading out the door, so if you don't mind…" Yancey's reasonable intervention was cut off by a whimpering sound that neither man would have heard if not for lupine hearing.

"Myles!" Ashley cried out before her squeal was cut off abruptly.

"Timmons!" Myles snarled, lifting the man by his uniform shirt. "When I'm finished, I'm going to kill you, revive you, and kill you again!" He tossed the Sheriff away, hearing the man's wrist snap when the large lawman landed. Myles had already turned toward the playground and the street bordering it.

Yancey headed around behind the building, transforming when he was out of sight of the school's windows. His heart in his throat, Myles raced across the blacktop, around agitated teachers and whimpering children.

Both werewolves converged on a fenced dumpster area behind the cafeteria. As soon as Myles registered the fact that one man, Del, was climbing a fence, Yancey had leapt up and sunk his teeth into the back of his arm.

Yancey and the large blonde man fell to the ground causing the chain link fence to undulate wildly. Myles was looking around frantically for Ashley when her fear-strained voice choked out his name.

"Myles," came her whispered rasp.

When he looked up, Myles thought his heart would explode. He felt the cold rush of anger and adrenaline upon seeing Al Washington hovering over his tiny mate, holding a knife to her throat.

The wiry little man turned to glare at Myles and his lush lips curved in a smug grin. Myles felt a blast of hatred when he saw Al twitch his knife causing a whimper from Ashley and a gush of blood from the resulting thin cut on her throat.

"Shh, Princess," he soothed from below, "hang on and I'll get you."

He heard the sound of her reassured sigh even through the taunting laughter of her captor. Vaguely, he noticed the other man whining and Yancey snarling as he gauged the distance from where he stood on the ground to where Ashley needed him to be.

"You'll get her!" Al snorted in disbelief. Turning back to the frightened girl he shouted, "Move, ya little bitch!" He raised his leg behind her and kneed her in the thigh.

"Don't!" Ashley snapped at him angrily, tears dripping down her cheeks as she clung to the fence.

He turned his head more fully toward her and leered, "You'll say don't one time before I…"

The impact of a large weight caused the fence to ripple and wave, the jingling and ringing of ten feet of stainless steel links so loud that nothing could be heard above the noise.

Myles let his presence speak for itself.

Al began to sweat and beg as he edged clumsily along the fence and away, swaying and swearing. Myles ignored him, reaching a muscled arm out to Ashley.

"C'mon Princess. C'mere. I have you now, sweet," Myles crooned, scooping an arm over her back.

His voice seemed to release her from the frozen fear and she leaned toward him, wrapping her arms around his neck as soon as he pulled her to his chest.

"Myles, Myles, Myles, Myles," she chanted, as if in prayer.

He cupped her head in his hand, pressing her face into the crook of his neck and shoulder and jumped to the ground. Loathe to release her, he wrapped both arms around her and stalked to where Yancey straddled Del, snarling into the big man's face.

"Go collect the trash, Yancey," Myles growled, not letting go of Ashley. "I'll stand on this git for you."

"She okay?" Yancey asked, edging off of Del.

Myles rubbed his cheek on the top of her head and kissed her. "She'll do," he said, hugging the small girl more tightly. He looked down at the man under his foot and snarled baring his teeth, fully aware of his frightening appearance.

Del blanched and clutched at the gravelly pavement under his hands, staring fixedly at the dark-haired man. Yancey nodded once and padded away. Within a minute, Myles heard the jingle of the fence accompanied by a strangled scream. He felt his grin widen as he stared at Del. The big man began to cry.

Chapter 15

Tracey carefully pulled the door closed as she stepped into the living room of Tav's house. With her own house full of werewolves for one more day, the couple was grateful for the gift of privacy awarded them in this second house.

Tav had been waiting for her here while she soothed her children to sleep. It had been a long week dealing with Jack and his cohorts. Although things were still strained between Myles and the Sheriff, some semblance of normalcy had been achieved. The convicts had been sent to a Federal prison on charges of kidnapping, the murder of Rusty, and the attempted murder of Tracey and her children. Everyone would be notified if there was to be a trial. Tracey had the courage to deal with it all now and would talk to her parents real soon to let them know everything was better now.

Earlier in the evening the entire entourage had gone to watch Ashley sing and dance in the school play. Her performance had been flawless but she'd broken down in a puddle of tears afterward, knowing that Myles was leaving the next day.

While Tracey knew her little girl loved all of her new family, she recognized that Ashley had a special bond with Myles. She didn't know how she felt about that, exactly. Not great, to say the least. But, it didn't matter tonight. The children were asleep and she had a very handsome man of her own right in front of her.

"Can little Tavist come out to play?" she whispered with a teasing smile.

"Mmm, maybe later," Tav mumbled, seated at his desk. "I'm drawing a picture, wanna see?"

Surprising her, he held out a pastel sketch of a beautiful woman with flowing hair and a come-hither look on her face. *Is that how he really sees me?* A bolt of desire shot through her as she looked at the picture. She felt sexy through and through.

"Hmmm," Tracey considered him, eyes narrowed. "Drawing a picture, huh? That sounds like more fun than what I had in mind."

"What did you have in mind?" Tav rumbled, moving from his chair to stand a few feet in front of her.

"Freeze tag," she giggled.

"Um, how about naked tag?" he closed the distance between them in a lunge, catching her against his chest and covering her mouth with his.

Tracey moaned and sunk one hand into his thick, soft hair. Her other hand moved down his muscled back, sliding over his toned and rounded buttocks. She moved both hands to his rear end and squeezed firmly, pulling him against her pelvis at the same time.

She was rewarded with a growl and felt his cock swell against her, hard and throbbing. His lips moved over hers, searing and hot, his tongue sliding across her lower lip, followed by nipping and nibbling teeth.

Before she could catch her breath, he swung her into his arms, gently chewing on her throat and shoulder. Tav nipped and chewed, lathed and kissed her from her neck down sending spikes of pleasure rippling through her.

Tugging and tearing, they managed to remove piece after piece of clothing until warm skin moved and stroked over warm skin. They stumbled backward, grappling and grunting as the fire that licked their bellies continued to blaze hotter and higher.

Tracey felt her rear end bump up against the edge of the desk and realized that she'd pulled Tav along with her during their erotic game of "naked tag". While she tried to find the lungpower to proclaim him "it", big hands gripped her hips and lifted her onto the desk.

He parted her legs with a nudge and slid in between them. He tilted her hips back aligning his burning erection with her hot feminine core.

"*Ohh*! Oh, Tavist!" She groaned, clutching at him and pulling him into her.

With a strong tug and thrust, Tav pulled her onto him, groaning as loudly as she did.

"Me!" he groaned. "Only ever me!"

"Yes!" she answered him, "Only you!" she moaned.

"Laughing, playing, working, only me, Tracey!" he half pled, half growled at her.

Breathing deeply, Tracey inhaled his soapy, sweaty, musky wild animal scent.

"Only you, Tavist," she whispered, nodding.

Locking eyes with her, Tav slowly pulled his hips back and thrust forward. Her breath hitched and she groaned. Still looking deeply into her eyes, he pulled out again, one centimeter at a time and then thrust in again.

Sensual hunger clawed at her. The friction of his thick, throbbing sex moving in and out of her was excruciating. The heat zipped through her and Tracey sunk all ten of her fingernails into his back and told him, "Do it. Don't tease me. You're *it*!"

All at once he snapped, rocketing forward and pounding into her forcefully. She wrapped her arms and legs around him and hung on, carried away by the wanton and starving animal that had moved into her body.

She heard someone mewling and moaning and realized somehow that she was the one crying out frantically. Tav seemed incapable of no more than inarticulate growls now and she heard herself begging him not to stop, anything but that.

With the force of an explosion, her climax hit and she screamed, the sound drowned out by Tav's roar of completion. For a moment or two, all she could feel was the shock of her explosion and his, reverberating through her body.

With a soft groan, Tav sunk to the floor, pulling her off the desk and on top of him. For long minutes, neither said a word, letting their sweat soaked bodies cool and their thundering hearts slow to a normal rhythm.

"Tavist?" she whispered after a while.

"Hmm?" he opened one eye.

"What *was* that?" her voice still sounded awestruck.

"Mmm," he grinned lazily. "That's how good we are together."

"Oh," she mused, turning it over in her mind. "Thought so," she grinned, fading to sleep with his warm chuckle chasing goosebumps across her heart.

The End